Taking the Lead

Michele L. Rivera

This is a work of fiction. Names, characters, places, businesses, organizations, and incidents either are a product of the author's imagination or are used fictitiously. Any resemblance to actual persons, living or dead, events, or locales is entirely coincidental.

Text copyright © 2013 by Michele L. Rivera

All Rights Reserved

First Paperback Edition

ISBN 978-0-9912666-1-6

Something of magnetic force pulled me closer to the girl,
It was strange and familiar
Crossing the boundaries of linear-
In the shadows I used to watch her lush lips spill secrets
And it made me ache in the spaces I could not deny existed
Except, of course, in dreams
She moved forward
I clumsily stepped back, in cloaks of shameful longing,
I planned escaping this attack
But she knew,
entering my thoughts like only girls can do-
She sealed the distance between us
her touch burned my skin
I would never be the same
On the outside or within
For passing years and countless nights and days
She was my home; we both promised we would stay-
This is where the passion ignites the flames of fear
When she renders me powerless; drowning in the tears
You see, that's the thing about a girl,
Her kisses leave you breathless
Her eyes become your world
But it never seems to matter where she stops, lingers or starts
She'll sometimes revive it,
sometimes break it,
but she will always steal your heart

Chapter One

"What do you think it feels like when your mind has decided to betray your body?" Micah asked her best friend, Emily, as if the question were as insignificant as the weather conditions outside.

Emily never looked up from flipping through the CD case creatively decorated by Micah with quotes from her favorite authors and celebrities. "Why don't you invest in an MP3 player like the rest of society instead of wasting your money on CDs?"

"CDs are our generation's version of what records are like for our parents. If I give up CDs then what's next? Giving up books?" Micah asked, lying on her bed, staring up at the ceiling. The ivory paint had begun to peel.

"Yes, books. That's why people are buying e-readers and tablets, because they can download books instead of lug them around. Soon you'll be the only one at the library. Micah, I worry about you," Emily joked, looking up at Micah from where she sat on the floor, her back against Micah's desk.

"Don't waste your worries on me, Em. I'll be fine. I actually like the feeling of holding a book and the smell of its pages. I don't know."

"The smell of old books? Mmm, sexy. You should bottle that and see how well it sells." Emily laughed.

Micah sighed. "Please, Emily, will you answer my question?"

"Dude, I didn't even understand your question. Just ask it in a more normal way. What are you trying to communicate, oh-so-poetic one?"

"You're my friend, right?" Micah asked, now sitting up.

Emily put down the case of CDs to meet her friend's frightened eyes.

"Yes, Micah. Of course I'm your friend. What's going on with you?"

"I have something to tell you," Micah said in a low tone.

Emily and Micah had known each other since first grade. Now they were both eighteen years old, in their senior year of high school, and still inseparable. They knew everything about each other and this only strengthened their connection. When a lot of their other friends from earlier years fell into different crowds, they stuck together. Micah wondered if that would always be the case.

"I'm listening," Emily responded.

"It's about that new girl in my English class."

Emily's eyes bulged. "Ooooo. I love it! Did you see something online?"

"No. It hasn't been posted online nor will it be! Promise?" Micah's voice was stern.

"Jeez, I promise." Emily clapped eagerly. "Now spill! What's that chick's name again anyway? She's a little…different."

Micah involuntarily twitched. "Her name is Casey."

"Oh yeah. Casey. Okay, so what about her?"

"Wait," Micah said, sitting up straighter. "Why do you think she's different?"

Emily shrugged. "I don't know. I can't explain it. It's just this vibe or whatever that I get from her. Besides, I've heard things."

"Online?" Micah asked, trying to sound as calm as possible.

"No, not online. Just from kids at school."

"What have you heard?" Micah perused her CD case to feign aloofness.

"You really haven't heard?" Emily asked. "And can we just pick a CD for crying out loud!"

Micah handed her friend the latest album she had purchased. "Here, put this one in."

"Sweet." Emily grinned, took the disc from Micah, and inserted it into the CD player.

"Emily, hello? Are you even paying attention? What have you heard?"

Emily bobbed her head to the music filling the room. "Look, I just heard she kind of, like, has a thing for *other* people."

Throat dry, Micah spoke hoarsely. "What do you mean '*other* people'?" She paused. "What, does she crush on werewolves or something?" Micah tried to joke but her panicked voice shook.

Emily sighed heavily. "Micah, I don't even have a class with Katie."

"Casey," Micah corrected. The sound of the name alone was enough to elevate Micah's heart rate.

Emily raised an eyebrow and continued, "Whatever. Casey. As I was saying before I was rudely interrupted, I don't have a class with her and even *I* can tell."

"Tell what? What can you tell? What are you getting at?"

"She sort of plays for the other team."

"What?" Micah fumbled. "What does that even mean?"

Emily chuckled. "Wow. With all those books you read, one would think you'd be a bit more enlightened."

Micah regained some of the feeling in her body, and swung a pillow at Emily, hitting her square in the face. "There, that's for you."

Emily snatched the end of the pillow that hit her. She tried to engage Micah in a game of tug of war, but Micah let go.

"It means she likes girls, Micah."

Micah stopped breathing. She stared blankly at her friend.

"Dude, you okay?" Emily asked. "I thought most people had heard that one."

Micah shook her head. "I…I didn't…I don't…no one has said anything to me."

Emily looked at Micah quizzically. "Okay. You started this conversation so what were you going to tell me about her? I thought maybe that was it."

Micah shook her head again. "Uh, no. I forget what I was going to tell you. I'll think of it eventually."

"Liar! Micah, you're such a bad liar, so give it up already. What about—" A slow, unexpected grin played across Emily's lips and her index finger pointed at Micah. "You!" she accused. "Oh. My. God. Micah, oh my god!"

Micah's eyes welled up as she waited for the world to dissolve.

Emily jumped up excitedly and scanned the walls of Micah's room, the room she had spent nearly every afternoon in for most of her life. She observed all the posters of beautiful female celebrities, Micah's so-called "role models." Emily let out one loud, "Finally!"

Micah put up both hands as if she were trying to stop traffic. "Shh!" She didn't want her mother to investigate Emily's uproar. "Wait. What do you mean, 'finally'?" Micah asked.

Emily's eyes shifted. "What? Oh, nothing." Her expression sobered. "Micah, just say it already. I can't handle the suspense anymore."

Micah said nothing.

Emily gave her a moment to think. "Ooookay. Let's try again. Micah, are you trying to tell me you maybe also play for another team?"

Micah began to cry hysterically. "You hate me," she groaned through sobs.

Emily sat beside Micah on the bed and took her friend's head, placing it on her lap. Emily stroked Micah's hair and kept repeating, "Shh, it's okay. I don't hate you."

Micah's wailing ceased to a sniffle. "I got snot on your jeans." Her breathing started to regulate. She rose. "Em, I'm gay. You're cool with that?" Micah croaked.

Emily's head tipped to the side. "And I'm a Gemini. Are you cool with that?" They smiled at each other. Emily pinched her lips together and then released them. "I won't tell anyone."

"There's more." Micah bowed her head.

"Micah, you're killing me here. This is like our own after school movie special. What the hell are you gonna tell me now? That you're a lesbian vampire or something?" Emily laughed at her own sense of humor. Micah's tension eased.

"Okay." Micah took a deep breath. "We kissed."

Emily's mouth dropped. "Your first kiss and you're just telling me NOW?"

"SHHH." Micah cupped her hand over Emily's mouth. "My mom cannot know. Besides, it just happened Monday."

Emily removed Micah's hand from her mouth. "Uh, it's Wednesday. That's one day too many of keeping your bestie in the dark." Emily glanced again at the huge poster of a scantily clad musician and smiled. "Go figure," she mumbled to herself and then looked over at Micah. "Do you want to talk about it?"

Micah gaped. "You aren't grossed out?"

"A kiss is a kiss is a kiss. Doesn't matter who it's with," Emily reassured.

Micah hugged her tightly. "I love you. Not like in a lesbian way though."

"Aww, of course you love me. I'm awesome. Now tell me about your first kiss."

Micah blushed, knowing she'd have to provide all the details because that was their promise to one another. Their bond was unbreakable and now, once again, there were no secrets between them.

Emily got off the bed to lower the volume of the stereo and sat back down. "Micah, before you tell me the goodies, can I ask you something?"

"What, spilling my guts to you isn't enough?" Micah scoffed.

"Well, how long have you known, you know, that you liked girls?" Emily was not sure how to phrase the question appropriately.

Micah's shoulders went up and down slowly, in rhythm with her breathing. "Since Monday? Since the kiss, I guess. I'm not really sure. It's like I was feeling things I didn't want to feel." Micah stared down at the floor. "I don't want to be different, Emily."

Emily frowned. "You're not different." Emily let this statement settle and started again. "Okay, so you're a little different but only a tiny bit. That's all." A song ended and there were a few seconds of silence before the next one began. "Does this have to do with that strange question you asked me earlier about your body and your mind and all that craziness?" Emily asked. "Because there's nothing to be ashamed of. Look, what about that talk show host? She's gay and she's cool."

Micah stared at her friend. "Gee, now I feel so much better."

"Hey, I'm trying to help."

Micah nodded. "I know, thank you. It's just that everything happened so fast. And yes, it's sort of like my mind knows it should want guys, but my body wants something else. I have no control over it. I'm an alien!"

"Okay, take it easy. You're not an alien. Who the hell says you should like guys? Your mom? Society? Since when are you one to even care what other people think? If you cared, you would have an MP3 player." There was a quiet laughter between them.

"I'm scared, Em."

"Micah, I kinda get that." A shadow crossed Emily's face.

"What's wrong?" Micah asked.

Emily gathered herself quickly. "Nothing…I want to hear about the damn kiss!"

There was something about Emily's disposition that Micah couldn't quite decipher. *Does she really want to know or is she just being polite?*

"Emily, I'd rather not talk about the kiss. It's *private.*"

"Errr fiiiiine. I just have two questions that you can answer with a simple yes or no. How's that?"

Micah delayed her response by blowing her nose into a tissue. "Okay."

"Perfect!" Emily studied Micah. "Did she kiss you?"

Micah dissected the remains of the tissue. "Yes."

"And did you like it?"

After a long hesitation, Micah answered, "Yes."

"Look at me," Emily requested.

Micah slowly moved her head so that she faced Emily. "What?"

"You are totally trying to hide a smile right now!" Emily squealed smugly.

Micah let her smile grow to its fullest. "Of course I liked it! Have you *seen* Casey? But I felt so bad after."

"Micah, I will keep telling you this for as long as I have to. There is nothing to feel bad about."

"Okay. It happened after school. Behind the library. I sort of ran away after the kiss," Micah confessed, her voice suddenly sad.

Emily shook her head. "Why?"

"Dude, I was scared and felt guilty and confused and I freaked out and told her I had to go. I told her I didn't like girls *that way*."

"But you *do*."

"Yeah, I *know*," Micah said with frustration. "Now I don't know how to fix it."

"Well, do you like her?"

Micah's voice wobbled. "Yes. I do."

"So talk to her. Tell her the truth," Emily suggested softly.

Emily had started pulling at a loose string on her shirt.

"Em, you okay?"

Emily looked up and blinked deliberately. She gave Micah a tired smile. "Sorry, I was just thinking. About how to help."

"It's fine. I've accepted that I've ruined it."

Emily stood up and wagged her finger. "Uh uh, you did not ruin it. This can be fixed."

Micah looked questioningly at her friend. "How? Emily, I'm not like you. I can't just go up to her and start talking. I hurt her feelings, I think."

"Do you trust me?" Emily asked.

"Most of the time," Micah admitted.

"Thanks a lot." Emily placed her hands on her hips. "Will you trust me?"

"Okay, fine. I'll trust you. Do you have a plan of action already in place?"

"No, but I'll come up with something. I just need some time."

Chapter Two

Thursday morning Micah's alarm sounded louder than usual, blaring that week's number one chart topper. It was the first night all week that she actually had a restful sleep. She had her best friend to thank for that. However, the idea of Emily trying to "fix" things with Casey was already gnawing at her.

After showering and pouring herself some cereal, Micah plopped down at the kitchen table across from her mother. She could tell she was being stared at so she looked up from her bowl, meeting a concerned gaze.

Mrs. Williams cleared her throat. "Good morning."

Micah gave her mom a tight-lipped smile. "Good morning."

"Micah, we need to talk," her mother stated flatly after taking a sip of coffee.

"'bout what?" Micah tried to sound nonchalant, but trepidation was emerging again.

"Well, we can get into it more when you get home from school today, but I feel as though you don't talk to me about things the way you once did. We aren't as close as we used to be, you know? I miss that. Micah, I miss you."

Micah sighed and rolled her eyes as far back as they could go, relying on disinterest to conceal her anxiety. "Mom, seriously? I'm older now. It's normal that I don't want to share everything with you. Can we please not have this conversation?" Micah feared that time alone with her mother would lead to the imminent unveiling of her recent dishonesty.

"Excuse me. I am the mother here and I will say what conversations we can and cannot have. I'd like to know what's going on with my daughter. Is that so wrong?" Her mom fidgeted with her coffee mug. "I was thinking we could go out for ice cream or something later and chat."

"Fine, whatever. And then will you leave me alone?"

"Let's just see how it goes today, okay?"

"Okay."

Her mom stood up, put her mug in the sink, then walked over and kissed Micah on the top of her head. "Great. I will see you back here at home around 3:30. And no, Emily cannot tag along. This is time for you and me, okay?"

"Yes, Mother." Micah waited as her mom gathered her purse and keys. She heard the front door shut then listened for the engine of her mother's car. When she was sure the car had pulled away, a few tears leaked down her face. "I miss you too, Mom," she whispered. She took a deep breath, picked up her bag, and headed for the bus stop.

The bus wound through the neighborhoods for an eternal fifteen minutes. A disheveled man was whistling loudly to no one in particular. A woman was trying to pacify a whimpering toddler. An agitated passenger was bickering with the driver about the fare. One of those MP3 players that Emily was constantly raving about would be convenient right about now. She latched onto the steel post and readied herself for the day. Thankfully, English, the only class she shared with Casey, was first period so she could get any potential confrontation over and done with.

Just as the bus pulled up to the school, it began to rain.

"Fabulous," Micah mumbled as she made her way to the entrance. She was using her backpack to take cover when suddenly there was an umbrella above her. She looked up, letting her bag down around her shoulders again, only to see Casey holding the umbrella over both of them. The heat rose in Micah's cheeks as she stared.

"Um, you're welcome," Casey teased.

"Thanks," Micah said barely above a whisper.

"Look, your friend said you wanted to talk so I thought I'd catch up with you before class."

"My friend?"

Casey smiled. "Yes, you know, friends. The people you associate with. They kind of resemble humans. I think you mentioned having a few."

This blush is just getting worse. No need for make-up here. Micah nodded. "Ah yes, friends. What friend told you that?" Micah already knew the answer. She revoked her earlier gratitude towards Emily.

"I come to school early on Thursdays for indoor track practice and busted your little sidekick taping a note to my locker. Not the most subtle thing ever, but hey."

"Friggin' Emily," Micah grumbled as it dawned on her that Emily met with her math tutor before class every *Thursday* morning.

"Excuse me?" Casey asked.

"Nothing, I'm sorry. I didn't need to talk to you. She was probably just playing around. She's a kidder, that Emily," Micah said, trying to sound light-hearted while secretly plotting Emily's death. Precisely at that moment, Emily, on her way to homeroom, walked behind Casey and gave Micah a thumbs up. Micah's eyes widened in distress.

"Oh, so it was a joke? You don't want to talk to me? You don't have anything to say?"

Micah shook her head. "Um. No, I can't think of anything. Sorry about the misunderstanding."

The halls emptied. "We should get to our homerooms," Casey said, looking down at her shoes while moving closer to Micah. Micah's heart raced as she was backed into the wall. Once Micah was fully against the bricks, Casey stared right into her eyes. In a panic, Micah surveyed the hallways to ensure no one was watching. She found herself unable to breathe. *What if I exhale? Did I brush my teeth this morning?* Casey smiled casually. "Well, if you happen to think of whatever it was you wanted to talk to me about, you know where to find me."

"I do?" Micah asked.

"Micah, I see you walking by my classes. I think you know my schedule better than I do."

Dear Earth, if you can hear me, now would be a good time to swallow me whole.

Casey laughed and gave her a little nudge. "Get to class, creeper," she said and walked away.

Micah hit her head against the wall repeatedly for a few seconds and then trudged to homeroom. So maybe she did know Casey's schedule. But that was for protection, so she could avoid her. And she didn't know Casey came to school early on Thursdays. *THAT would've been useful information*, she thought to herself.

After homeroom, Micah headed off to English, hoping that maybe Casey would decide to skip class. She took her seat and opened up *Othello* to the chapter the class was studying. Micah paid no attention to the lesson as she had read *Othello* on her own two years ago.

Just before the bell rang, Casey snuck into her seat two rows over from Micah. Between them sat Samantha Stevenson, a girl who rarely attended class and was often ridiculed for dressing in band tee shirts from the '90s. Mostly Samantha was notorious for trying to get the class to partake in peace rallies. Thankfully, Samantha *was* in class today to keep the distance between Micah and Casey.

Samantha suddenly leaned over to Micah and handed her a piece of paper. "Casey told me to give you this," she explained. Micah looked over at Casey, who winked at her. Micah shifted uncomfortably. "Thank you, Samantha," she said.

Samantha nodded and started drawing sketches on her notebook. Micah wasn't sure why people made fun of Sam so often. She seemed nice enough.

Micah examined the piece of paper and opened it. It was a glimmering stamp of Casey's lips. Flustered, Micah quickly put the paper in her pocket and glared over at Casey, who smiled proudly before turning her attention to the teacher. Micah tore out a page from her own notebook and scribbled down, "After class I need a word."

She leaned over to Samantha. "Psst. Samantha."
Samantha sized her up curiously. "Yes?"

"Can you please give this to Casey?" Micah asked.

"You can call me 'Sam.' Give me the note."

Micah held out the paper. "Thanks, Sam. By the way, I like your shirt."

Samantha's eyes glinted. "You know who this band is?"

"Of course! I just saw them perform live about a month ago," Micah said excitedly, as the band's talent was an ongoing debate between her and Emily.

Sam took the paper and smiled. She passed it over to Casey. Then she leaned back towards Micah and tipped her head inconspicuously in Casey's direction. "Just so you know it's kind of obvious." Micah's face crimsoned. Samantha continued, "I don't judge. I won't tell anyone."

Micah nodded in petrified silence. She watched Casey open the note and read it, and then Casey met her eyes and smiled.

Finally the bell rang to end class and Micah waited in the hall for Casey. Casey stepped through the doorway and over to where Micah was standing.

"What the hell do you think you're doing?" Micah whispered harshly and flung her arms in the air.

"Trying to make you sweat," Casey said with a smirk.

Micah glowered.

"I'm kidding! Look, whether or not this morning's message was a joke, I think we *should* talk. I think you have something to tell me."

Micah let out a breath of disbelief. "Oh really? And what could that be? Since you seem to know everything?"

"I'm being serious. Will you just meet me after school?"

"I can't. I have to go right home. I have a date."

Casey's eyes widened. "With who?"

"Uh, my mom. We're going out for ice cream."

Casey laughed. "Goober. Okay, well, can you call me when you get home from your…date?"

"I'll think about it." Micah walked away, failing terribly at her attempt to exude confidence.

Lunchtime finally rolled around. Micah rehearsed on the way to the cafeteria. She would thank Emily for opening up a dialogue between her and Casey, and then she would berate Emily for humiliating her. Before Micah could finalize her agenda, Emily came up beside her in the lunch line and tapped her on the butt.

"Hey, buddy," Emily said happily, eyes wide with anticipation.

"Don't even," Micah grumbled.

"Oh, come on! Was it that bad?"

Micah stared her best friend down. "How the hell did you know she came to school early on Thursdays? How come you didn't tell me? I was totally ambushed!"

Emily placed a hand on each one of Micah's shoulders. "Breathe," she commanded. "Listen, I didn't tell you because I didn't know her whereabouts were important to you until last night. Then I figured that it worked to my advantage so that I could help you out," Emily explained calmly.

Micah shook her head. "I really wish you didn't do that."

Emily smiled. "Do you? Do you really wish that? Aren't you just a tiny bit happy that you might have a chance to clear the air?"

"I told Casey that my *ex*-best friend made a mistake and that I didn't need to tell her anything."

"Why?" Emily exclaimed. "Why do you continue to kill me this way? Just talk to the girl. Tell her what you want to tell her."

"You make it sound so easy."

"Micah, it *is* that easy," Emily said, looking up at the lunch lady. "Ham and cheddar, please." Emily turned her attention back to Micah.

"And you?" the lunch lady asked Micah impatiently.

"Same," Micah answered. She looked over at Emily. "Em, she wants to talk after I get back from my date with my mom today."

Emily laughed. "You have a date with your mom?"

"Why does everyone find that so funny?" Micah wondered.

"No reason. So are you going to call?" Emily asked. "You should call."

"I don't know. I don't really have anything to open this conversation with, you know, like a conversation piece," Micah fretted.

The girls walked towards their lunch table and passed by Casey, who was sitting with her friends from track. Just as Casey went to take a sip of water, Emily bumped herself into Casey's chair, causing the water to spill all over Casey's shirt. Casey looked up quickly as Emily was running away.

Micah froze, horrified. "Uh, sorry about that." She gave Emily, who was sitting at their table already, a look of pure dismay.

Casey nodded. "Really?" She stood up to face Micah. People began to quiet and turn their attention to Casey and Micah. Some moron jumped up and yelled, "Girl fight!" and some people cheered. Micah hadn't the faintest idea of what to do to remedy this situation. Casey took Micah's tray from her and placed it on a table. She grabbed Micah's arm and hauled her out of the cafeteria.

"Ouch," Micah complained about the grip Casey had on her. "Where are we going?" Micah asked as she looked back at Emily, whose eyes were practically coming out of her head.

Casey ushered Micah into the girls' bathroom. "You are going to help me clean off my shirt."

Micah swallowed hard. "It's just water."

Casey nodded in agreement. "Uh huh. Water that *you* spilled all over me or was that a prank, too?"

"Look, Casey, it's Emily. She wants me to talk to you so she's being stupid," Micah faltered.

Casey pushed Micah into a stall and locked it. *What's happening?*

"Do you want to or not?" Casey asked.

Micah didn't move a muscle. "Do I want to what?"

"Talk," Casey stated, "because I really think you have something you want to tell me. Yes or no? Why does your friend want you to talk to me? If you don't tell me then I will ask her myself."

Micah didn't like that option. "Okay, okay. I wanted to tell you something."

"Continue," Casey requested.

"Look, Casey, I'm sorry. I'm sorry about the water and I'm sorry about the kiss."

Casey was close. Micah could pinpoint the brand of her shampoo. It was then that she diagnosed herself with claustrophobia.

Casey sighed. "Why are you sorry about the kiss?"

Should Micah answer truthfully? "Because I—"

"Did you like it and that's why you're sorry? Because you liked it and you got scared and pushed me away? Is that why? Well?"

For a moment, Micah was captivated by how beautiful she thought Casey was. It was hard not to check out the way Casey's wet tee shirt clung to her.

"I don't know if I liked it." *Lie*, Micah scolded herself. Then she felt the warmth of Casey's hand against her cheek. Casey's dark brown eyes were completely focused on Micah as she leaned in. Micah closed her eyes as the heat of Casey's mouth pressed against her own. Micah wholly succumbed to the rapture. Casey slowly backed away.

"Sorry. I wanted to refresh your memory. So, now do you know if you liked it or not?"

Micah's respiratory system hadn't recovered from the kiss. "Look, I liked it. I like you…but I can't do this."

"Do what? Be with me?" Casey asked.

On the verge of tears, Micah replied, "I can't, Casey. People will know and I can't *not* care about what they say. Not about this. I'm sorry."

"You sure are sorry about a lot of things, huh?" Casey said as she let herself out of the stall.

"Wait! How did you know what time I was going to be coming into school? And how did you know I wouldn't have an umbrella and you were so prepared?" Micah asked.

Casey came back and took a deep breath. She cupped Micah's face with her hands. "I'm a creeper, too. I listen to the weather and you mentioned before that you don't believe in umbrellas."

"They always blow inside out," Micah complained.

Casey smiled. "Look, cutie, I want to be with you, but you need to figure out your shit." And just like that, she left. Micah stood there as the bell rang ending lunch period and she felt her stomach rumble. *This day just keeps getting better*, she thought.

After school, Micah went prowling for Emily. She had to get home for quality time with her mom, but she needed to tear into Emily first.

Emily finished putting her books away, and slammed her locker shut as Micah came storming at her. "Whoa, hey, calm down. How did it go?"

Micah pulled on her own hair. "Emily, this is crazy! You can't do stuff like that. It was insane! Do you understand me? One more stupid thing like that and we are not friends anymore." Micah hyperventilated.

Emily steered her friend into a secluded alcove of the hallway and wrapped her arms around her. "Micah, I'm sorry. You said you needed some help starting a conversation, so I was trying to help."

Micah looked up at Emily in disbelief. "You thought that dumping water all over her would be helpful? Dysfunctional much?"

Emily shrugged. "I'm one for dramatics," she said as she reached in her backpack and handed Micah something wrapped in a plastic bag.

"What's this?"

"Your sandwich. I thought you might be hungry," Emily said. "I'm sorry if I caused more trouble. It bugs me that you take no risks in life, like EVER, and I don't want to see you unhappy. You're my bestie."

Micah was too much of a softie to be angry any longer. "No more foolishness. It wasn't helpful."

Emily nodded. "Not helpful. Got it." She took two steps away, and then turned back. "And that smudge on your top lip really isn't your color." Emily grinned. "Call me later." She waved upon departure.

Micah frantically wiped the top of her lip with her shirtsleeve. She was dreading hanging out with her mom, wishing that she could spend more time talking to Emily about what happened. Was Emily right? Did she never take risks? Is unhappiness the outcome of playing it safe? For now, she was going to be a typical teenager and bask in her life's misery.

Chapter Three

Micah arrived home from school, defeated by the day's events. Her mom was there in the kitchen to greet her. *Of course.*

"Hi, honey," her mother said as she finished rummaging through the pile of mail on the counter. "How was your day?"

"Fantastic," Micah droned.

Her mom nodded. "I'll ask you again to please tone it down on the sarcasm. How was your day?"

Micah backtracked. Her mom was only trying to be nice. "Sure, Mom. Sorry about that. My day was alright."

"Good. Now, are you ready for some ice cream? We could go down to the local shop, or I heard about this new frozen yogurt place in the center. What do you think?"

"I vote for local."

"Okay, but one of these days you're going to have to start trying new things," her mom said as she grabbed her coat out of the closet.

You have no idea about what "new" things I've been trying, Micah thought.

"Where's your raincoat? Did you get soaked this morning?" her mother asked.

"No. I miraculously made it through the door just in time," Micah lied as she, too, plucked her jacket off the hanger.

Her mom dangled the car keys. "You want to drive?"

Micah's eyes lit up. "Seriously?" Micah had gotten her license just under a year ago. She could not yet afford a car of her own, and both of her parents were still averse to being in the car with her when she was behind the wheel. *Stupid fire hydrant.* Her mom was trying to schmooze her for sure.

Micah swiped the keys. "Let's do this!"

They'd barely left the driveway before Micah was on the receiving end of an interrogation. She groaned inwardly as the cross-examination began.

"So, tell me. What's new with you?" her mother asked, shutting off the car radio.

Micah sighed. "Mom, really?"

"Yes, really."

"Fine. I was thinking about getting a job. I need more money so I can start saving for my own car. Babysitting for the Andersons here and there isn't helping me rake in the big bucks."

Micah's mom stared thoughtfully at her. "Have you seen anywhere you could apply? Somewhere within walking distance?"

Micah shrugged. "The Bean is hiring. The bus goes there and…free coffee!" *And Megan, the hot barista.*

"Well, then, you should apply. Seems like you have it all mapped out."

"Really? You support that idea?"

"Sure thing. You know how much I love coffee," her mom said, grinning.

Micah imagined taking yet another bus aside from the one she already took back and forth to school every day. She cringed, second-guessing her game plan.

"Okay, well maybe I'll think about it some more."

They arrived at the ice cream shop. Micah pulled into a parking space and got out. Mrs. Williams followed close behind as they went inside.

"Micah, you know that the plan is to sit here and eat *and* talk, right?"

Micah looked away from the menu board and at her mom. "Yes, I realize that."

The kid behind the counter taking orders was a senior she recognized from school. "Can I get you something?" he asked them.

Her mom smiled politely. "Yes, please. I will have a medium ice cream, half cookie dough and half triple fudge chocolate with extra chocolate sprinkles in a cone!"

The kid nodded and then looked at Micah. "What about you?" Micah pursed her lips. "I'll have a medium chocolate ice cream in a cup. Plain." The kid smiled and walked away.

Micah's mom clucked in disapproval.

"What?"

"This is what I meant earlier about trying new things. You've had nothing but chocolate ice cream since you were an infant *and* there is chocolate ice cream in the freezer at home."

Micah shrugged. "Whatever. It's what I like."

They got their ice creams and sat across from one another at a table in the corner of the shop, away from where most of the customers were congregated.

"Mom, how's your ice cream?" Micah asked, trying to be cordial.

"Absolutely delicious," her mom said, eyes rolling in the back of her head. "It's orgasmic."

"Gross, Mom! Don't say stuff like that," Micah pleaded, hoping that no one around them had heard what her mother said.

Her mom laughed as she swallowed another mouthful. "What? Because I'm old I can't say 'orgasm'?"

Micah's eyes grew wide with horror. "Mom, please, I'm begging you."

"Okay. You do know what an orgasm is though, right, sweetie? Because it's important to know," her mom stated matter-of-factly.

Micah shook her head. "Yes, Mom, I know. Can we please talk about something else, because it creeps me out when you talk about certain stuff."

Micah's mom looked at her with curiosity. Micah did not like this look. "What kind of stuff? Sex stuff?"

Micah was fortunate to have such laid-back parents, but she was feeling the disadvantages of that in this moment. "Yes, Mom, that stuff."

"How about we make a deal? If you agree to it, I'll stop talking about sex in public," her mom propositioned. Micah was immediately suspicious.

"What kind of deal?" Micah asked.

Her mom straightened. "I get to ask you one question and you must answer it honestly. Then we enjoy our ice cream and get out of here."

Hmm. Let's think about this. My grades are up. I haven't committed any felonies. Could she have heard me talking to Emily? Probably not. She's clueless. Freedom, here I come! "Fine. One question," Micah agreed.

Her mom nodded. "Are you a lesbian?"

Micah began choking on her ice cream. She should've given her mom more credit for being intuitive. She managed to ingest it. She scoped her surroundings squeamishly as her mom stood behind her, patting her on the back.

"Sweetie, are you okay?" her mom asked, returning to her chair once Micah's hacking stopped.

"Yes, I'm good. I'm great." Micah reclined, extended her legs, and folded her hands behind her head. "Everything is all good over here." After a fleeting pause, she rebounded and looked at her mom. "Why would you ask me that?"

"You can't answer a question with a question. If you want to leave, then you have to fulfill your end of the bargain," her mom said firmly.

"No, Mom. I'm not"—Micah looked around, leery of spectators, and then hunched over the table—"a lesbian."

Her mom stared at her. "Okay, because you and Emily have an awfully close relationship. I just wanted to put it out there, because your father and I would be completely accepting if you were a gay."

"A gay? What is that, Mom? People don't talk like that," Micah said, exasperated. But then it sunk in. "Wait, what? You thought Em and I were a thing? And you would be okay with it if we were?"

"Yes. You are our daughter and we'll support you no matter what."

This would be a good opportunity to let it all out, she told herself. "Mom, that's sweet, but Emily and I are just really good friends."

"I see. So are you a lesbian with anyone else?" her mother probed.

"Mom, you said one question and I answered you and this is extremely embarrassing."

Her mom cleared her throat. "Okay, well you're obviously unhappy that I asked, but a woman I work with is a lesbian. She has some unique ways about her. Kind of like you, that's all, so it got me thinking."

Micah snorted. "Oh. That's flattering. Thanks a bunch, Mom."

"Well, she's out and proud and all that," her mom said.

"Good for your friend, Mom, really."

"Micah, I'm just saying that I love you whether you have feelings for other women or men or both."

"Okay. I get it, but it's not what you think," Micah said as they stood up to leave. "Thanks for the ice cream and for supporting my heteronormativity."

Micah threw up in her mouth a little at the thought of dating boys. For the whole drive home she regretted being deceitful.

Micah and her mom arrived at their house to be greeted by Emily, who was sitting on the front steps.

"Emily, hello. Fancy seeing you here," Micah's mom said in mock incredulousness.

Emily's face wrinkled. "Um. You too?"

Mrs. Williams smiled at the girls and went inside.

Micah stood in front of Emily. "Hey. What's up?"

"I decided to come here and wait for you. My parents were fighting again." Emily rolled her eyes. "As soon as the rain stopped, I peaced out."

"So you're here to seek refuge?"

"Obviously," Emily said wryly.

"You wanna talk about it?"

"Nah. Same old crap. I'm good." Emily maneuvered herself up using the railing.

They entered the house and Emily continued talking. "Look, I'm really sorry about all the ridiculous things I did today. I wasn't trying to sabotage you. I really thought I was being helpful."

They reached Micah's room, and Micah shut the door as Emily sat on her bed. Micah sat beside her. "I know. I forgive you for being an idiot."

Emily smiled ruefully. "So, what was your date like with your mom and what happened in the bathroom at lunch?"

Micah hung her head and laughed a little. "In the bathroom, Casey kissed me and then got mad, because I told her I couldn't be with her. And then my mom took me out for ice cream and asked me if I were in a relationship with you."

Emily stared at Micah for a moment and they both began laughing. "Wow, that's a lot to take in," Emily said. "Wait, why did you tell Casey you couldn't be with her? And what did you tell your mom about us? Did you come out to her?"

Micah groaned. "I told my mom there wasn't anything going on between us. I'm not sure why, but I couldn't come out to her. As for Casey, I tried to explain my feelings and that didn't go over well. Em, you said it yourself that people can tell that she's gay. If I date her, everyone's going to start talking about me. I don't want to be the weirdo lesbian in our school. Knowing my luck, I'll come out and Casey will dump me. Then I'll be abandoned in lesbian land, tortured and alone."

"Jesus, Micah, depressing much?" Emily asked. "Lesbian land torture sounds like some kind of kinky porno," she added, laughing lightly.

Micah scrunched her nose. "Of course you would think of a porno. I'm just saying, what if that's my destiny?"

"Dude, you need to calm down. If people start running their mouths, I'll defend you."

"No offense, Em, but I'm all set with your help."

Emily smirked. "Okay, I can appreciate that. But seriously, Micah, you can't keep this inside forever. And you can't not be with the person you want to be with because you're afraid of what people are going to say. People are always going to say something, you know?"

"No, Em. I don't know," Micah said as she lay back on her bed. "I'm so confused."

Emily lay next to her. "I don't think you're confused. I think you're just scared and you need to have a little faith."

Micah looked at Emily, who held her gaze. "You're right, I'm scared," Micah admitted.

Emily thrust her arms into the air. "Ahhh! I think you should tell your mom the truth. She's cool! She'll get it." Emily let her limbs lax and they thudded into the mattress. "And I think you need to go after Casey before she gets away, because then you'll be kicking yourself in the ass that you didn't jump on that shit."

Micah let out a guttural sigh. "I'm not even sure I love her. I'm just really attracted to her."

"What? Who the hell says you have to be in love with someone to date them?" Emily shook her head and gave Micah a playful push. "How many times do I have to tell you? This is real life, not a romantic comedy."

Micah laughed as she sat up. "I envy you."

"Why?"

"You're so cavalier. About life. About everything."

"Look, Micah, I got your back. You won't be alone, but you have to eventually do something. Be brave for Christ's sake!" Emily catapulted off the bed, dislodged a stuffed animal from the top of Micah's dresser, and gleefully chucked it at her.

Micah salvaged the toy from where it had landed behind a barrel, and then stood upright. "I'll give it some thought."

Emily walked over to Micah and gave her a supportive shoulder squeeze. "Good."

"Do you want to stay for dinner?" Micah asked.

"No, thanks. I took some money off the kitchen table. My parents were too busy cussing each other out to notice. I'm going to get myself some sushi."

"Nasty. I don't know how you can eat that stuff."

Emily started laughing. "There are so many comments I could throw back at you right now about eating stuff, but I'm just not going to go there."

Micah threw Emily a dirty look and pointed to the door. "Out!" She tried to sound stern but couldn't help but smile. Emily waved and pranced from the room.

Micah ruminated on Emily's words for a moment, and then made her way downstairs.

Her parents were in the kitchen. Mr. Williams was cutting up some form of red meat and her mom was skimming the local newspaper.

Her dad glanced up as she approached. "Hey, honey, how are you? How was ice cream?"

Micah looked at her mother and then at her father. "Hey, Dad, I'm fine. Ice cream was good. How was your day?"

Mr. Williams nodded thoughtfully. "It was pretty good." He resumed cutting. "Roast beef tonight. You in?"

"Sure, so long as it's not still bleeding." Micah sat across from her mother. "Mom," she said quietly.

"Micah?" Mrs. Williams impersonated her daughter's tone.

"Can I invite a friend over for dinner tomorrow?"

"Sure. This means you have automatic dish duty though," her mom said, smiling.

"Aww, Mom," Micah whined, "I have dish duty tonight. Tomorrow is your night."

"Yes, but as the matriarch of this household, I can change the rules. So tomorrow night it is. Any requests?"

What does Casey even like? "How about something vegetarian?"

"Bummer," her dad mumbled. Micah shot him a look and he just smiled.

"I'll make my famous eggplant parm," her mom suggested.

Micah remembered the last time her mom made this meal. "Umm, how about something else?"

Her mother's rosy complexion clouded over. "Fine. Boxed mac and cheese it is."

"Great! Thanks, guys," Micah said and ran back upstairs. She sat down at her desk, picked up the phone, and began to dial. *Just breathe*, she told herself.

"Hello?" a voice answered.

"Hey, Casey, it's me. Look, I'm sorry about today. I would like the opportunity to make things right. Do you want to come over tomorrow for dinner? My mom's making homemade mac and cheese." Micah winced. *Why are you lying again?* she asked herself harshly.

There was a long pause. *Why isn't she saying anything? Maybe this was a bad idea.*

"Okay. What time?"

Micah exhaled. "How about six o'clock?"

"I'll be there. See you then," Casey said. She hung up the phone, leaving Micah with butterflies in the pit of her stomach and an extraordinary thirst she wasn't quite sure how to quench.

Chapter Four

Micah slid into her homeroom seat right before the bell Friday morning. Somehow, she managed to oversleep. The last thing she remembered was kissing in a dream. Everything had felt so right; a part of her must have wanted the dream to continue. Eventually, she heard her mom calling her name repeatedly, which caused her to awaken.

"Micah Williams?" The teacher was taking attendance.

"Here," she said flatly. *Barely*, she thought, trying to hold onto pieces of the dream.

The bell sounded for first period and Micah made her way down the hall. An arm swung around her.

"Good morning," Emily said cheerily.

Micah immediately brushed Emily's arm off her. "Hey. Good morning."

"What's wrong with you? Not one for the touchy feelies today?"

Micah shook her head. "Sorry, I was lost in a thought and you startled me."

"No worries. So, what do we have planned for tonight? I was thinking we could stream the best TV show EVER and order some pizza."

Micah's expression contorted. "Em, I kind of have plans. And don't you ever get sick of watching *Blonde Crusader*?"

Emily clutched her heart dramatically. "Okay, first of all, with who? And second, hell no! How can a person get sick of such a masterpiece? It's not possible."

"I took your advice and called Casey last night."

Emily's eyes widened. "And?"

"And she's coming over for dinner. My mom's cooking."

Emily frowned. "Is she making her eggplant thing?"

Micah laughed. "No, everything will be fresh out of the box."

"Phew," Emily said, laughing also. "That was a rough dinner."

Micah smiled. Emily had experienced Mrs. Williams's first attempt at cooking Italian food from scratch, too.

"Okay, I have to get to sociology class," Micah said, pointing down the hall.

"Alright. I'll see you later in history." Emily headed in the opposite direction.

"Emily," Micah called out to her.

Emily turned around. "What's up?"

"Are you mad? About tonight?"

"Are you kidding? I'm already stoked to get a phone call from you Saturday morning." Emily winked and continued down the hall. Relief washed over Micah.

Micah was counting down the minutes until school released, but every classroom's clock had a different time. Unfortunately, her watch was where she left it, which was on her dresser. According to her references, the current time was somewhere between 10:00 a.m. and 10:20 a.m.

Her mind wandered again to the remnants of last night's dream. *It just doesn't make sense.* She cursed at the clock. She was certain that not one of the hands had moved. An impure image of Casey invaded her thoughts. She shook her head. *I'm so gay.*

At last, the bell to end the period sounded off. Micah packed up her books and headed to history class.

As Micah walked down the hall, someone fell in step with her. Before she could look up, she heard his voice.

"Hey, Micah, how are you?" Jared Woods, a boy from her homeroom, asked.

Micah had only spoken to Jared on occasion and wasn't sure what he was doing conversing with her. Jared was considered one of the more popular boys in her grade. From what she had heard, he was also a star athlete.

"Um, hi, Jared. I'm okay. How are you?"

Jared smiled. "Look, I have something I want to ask you."

"Shoot," Micah said apprehensively.

"You and Emily Mathis are pals, right?" He shoved his hands deep into his jean pockets. *Why is he asking me about Emily?* Micah stared at his face. Jared was pretty good looking…for a boy.

"Yes. And you're asking me this why?"

Jared sighed. "Is she seeing anyone? I only ever see her around with you. But I don't want to assume she's single, because I'd look like an ass if I asked her out on a date and she were spoken for."

"And if she is single?"

"Well, then maybe you could put in a good word for me?"

Micah smiled. "Fine. But if you ask her out, you have to promise me that you'll treat her better than you have ever treated anyone ever in your life," she said sternly and stuck out her hand.

Jared grinned and shook her hand firmly. "I promise."

"This conversation never happened. Oh, and she likes Italian and Thai food. Bonus points if you can sit through an episode of *Blonde Crusader*."

"Cool. Is that the show with that hot chick, Sarah something?" he asked.

Micah shook her head. "Yes, but you might not want to tell Emily how 'hot' you think she is."

Jared thought about this and nodded. "Good call. Thanks a lot for your help, Micah," he said and headed in the other direction.

Micah was only one of a few students left in the hall. She jogged the remainder of the way to history.

Emily looked up when Micah entered the class. Their seats were side by side so note passing and gossiping quietly were fairly easy. Emily's eyebrow raised as Micah took her seat.

"What's up with you?" Emily whispered.

Micah mimicked Emily's facial expression. "What?"

"You look like you're keeping a secret."

"Jesus, can't I get anything by you?"

"For the last time, my name isn't Jesus." Emily found this hilarious. "And no, you can't, because your face is too expressive. You're an easy read."

Without warning, a flash from Micah's dream flooded her head again. Micah suddenly felt sick to her stomach with anxiety. She lost her train of thought and fell silent.

"Hello? Earth to Micah," Emily whispered.

"Huh? No, I'm here. What is it?"

"Dude, what's going on with you?" Emily asked again.

"Excuse me, Emily and Micah, is there something you would like to share with the class?" the teacher asked. All eyes fell on the two of them.

"No, sir, we were just discussing how much we loooove your teaching methods," Emily said and the class laughed.

The teacher smirked. "Emily, if I have to speak to you again, then you're staying after school. Understand?"

"I understand."

After Emily responded, Micah handed her a note. Emily unfolded it and stared at it for a long time. It read, "Jared Woods is going to ask you out. He asked me if you were available and I told him yes. Are you excited?"

After what seemed like an hour, Emily started scribbling words down on the paper and handed it back to Micah. All that was written on the paper were the words, "Cool, thanks."

They did not speak for the rest of the class. The bell rang and most of the kids bustled to the cafeteria. Micah waited for Emily to gather her books.

"Em, what's wrong? You think he's nice, right? Kind of a looker, no?" Micah asked.

Emily shrugged. "He's alright." She looked up to make sure no one else was around. "Listen, Micah, I think it's sweet that you're trying to set me up and stuff.

But I'm going through some things and I really don't feel like dating right now."

Not the reaction I had expected. "Oh. I didn't know stuff was going on." *What isn't she telling me?* "Do you want to talk about anything?"

Emily shook her head. "It's fine. Let it go." She grabbed her pile of books and left.

What the hell? Micah plodded to the lunch room alone.

Micah searched the cafeteria for Emily, but was unable to locate her. Micah sat down and stared at her lunch bag, not feeling hungry at all. There was a knock on the table. Micah looked up as Casey cruised by with her friends. She dazzled Micah with a smile and kept on going to where she routinely sat.

Micah sighed, clamped her water bottle, and began struggling to get it open. Suddenly it was taken out of her hands. Micah watched as Emily twisted the cap loose and took a seat next to Micah. Emily handed the bottle back to her.

"You're here," Micah said.

"Of course." Emily took a deep breath. "I'm sorry about earlier. I shouldn't have left you like that."

"It's okay. I'm sorry I tried setting you up without talking to you about it first."

Emily nodded. "Consider us even for the commotion I caused at lunch yesterday."

Micah smiled. "Hardly fair, but I'll take it." She took a long sip of water. "Do you want me to talk to Jared?"

Emily shook her head. "No. I got it. Don't worry."

Emily's mild demeanor, given the state of affairs, rattled Micah.

"Anyways, are you nervous about tonight? Do you need a pep talk?" Emily asked.

Micah's face distorted in agitation. "No! I'll be fine."

Emily smiled. "I'm sure you will be."

Chapter Five

Around 5:45 Friday evening, a marginal amount of sweat started to dribble from Micah's scalp. She sat at the kitchen table, staring at the door. Mrs. Williams stopped stirring the macaroni and cheese on the stovetop to look over at Micah.

"Sweetie, a little help would be nice," her mother said, nodding to the stack of plates in the center of the table. "The table isn't going to set itself."

Micah nodded catatonically. "Yeah, sure." She stood up and slowly began to put the plates down along with silverware and napkins.

"Are you okay?" her mother asked.

Micah looked up and met her mother's eyes. "Yes, I'm fine. I just feel bad about lying to Casey, telling her that you're making dinner from scratch."

Micah's mom shook her head and continued cooking. "Micah, fibbing gets you nowhere."

"Mom, I—"

"Happy Friday!" Micah's dad declared, coming through the door with a big smile. He kissed Micah on the forehead and went over to the stove to kiss Micah's mom on the lips.

"Gross," Micah joked. Her dad turned around and pointed his finger at her.

"Someday," he started, "you're going to want to come home to a—" There was a knock at the door. Micah felt relieved that her father couldn't finish that sentence, but completely unhinged at the idea of Casey standing just outside.

"Honey, can you get that? It's probably your friend Cathy," he said.

"Her name is Casey, Dad, Casey," Micah said and headed to the front of the house.

Be suave. She opened the door. Casey was standing there with a knapsack and a sleeping bag. Her smile was devious. Micah lost her breath. She pointed to the sleeping bag.

"Uhhh, why'd you bring that?"

Casey's eyes lit up. "Didn't you say this was a sleepover?"

The blood drained from Micah's face as a mix of panic and excitement swirled through her. She did her best to act naturally and motioned for Casey to follow her back to the kitchen.

"Hey, can Casey spend the night? We're going to watch some movies after dinner."

Her parents looked at one another and her mother nodded at her father. "Sure, sweetie," he said to Micah.

Micah reached over and grabbed Casey's hand. She pulled her towards where Mr. and Mrs. Williams were standing by the stove. Casey squeezed Micah's hand and let go.

"Mom, Dad, this is Casey."

Casey reached out and shook hands with Micah's dad and then her mom. "It's nice to meet you, Mr. and Mrs. Williams. I appreciate you letting me spend the night."

"It's nice to meet you too and you're welcome. Why don't you put your stuff upstairs? Dinner should be ready in a few minutes," Mrs. Williams said.

"That would be great," Casey said and turned to face a completely immobilized Micah. Casey raised her eyebrows at Micah.

"Oh, right. Yes, let's get your things upstairs," she stammered and started toward the staircase with Casey right behind her. *Stay calm*, she told herself.

Micah opened the door to her bedroom and pointed to a small, empty space near the dresser. "You can put your stuff over there for now."

Casey entered the room and softly closed the door behind her. Micah swallowed what felt like a rock. Casey gracefully walked across the room and put down her sleeping bag and knapsack. Casey's lip gloss made her lips look extra kissable. *Is kissable even a real word?*

"Can I help you?" Casey asked. Micah had been staring.

Micah pointed to the door. "Uh, we should get downstairs for dinner."

Casey looked around Micah's bedroom walls and then her eyes fell on Micah's bed. "So this is where she hides away."

Micah nodded. "Yes, this is my evil lair."

Casey chuckled. "Nice posters. You sure your parents don't know?"

"Know what?" Micah asked, trying to play it cool, and remembering Emily's recent reference to the bedroom décor.

Casey came over to where Micah stood. They were inches apart. "Seriously?" Casey asked.

"Okay. No, my parents don't know yet."

They held each other's gaze for a few moments. *You like her. Prove it!* Micah's heart began to beat rapidly and she took Casey's hand. She proceeded to run her thumb over Casey's fingers. Casey's eyes widened and then locked on their touching hands.

Micah inhaled sharply, leaned in, and brushed her lips across Casey's cheek. Casey took her hand back, placed it on the nape of Micah's neck, and tilted Micah's face closer to her lips. Casey kissed her and Micah felt an exhilarating unsteadiness, exactly like she had during every kiss before this one.

Micah stepped back and smiled when the kiss came to an end. "I figured it out."

"Figured what out?" Casey whispered back.

Micah smiled. "My shit." Casey started to laugh, and was caught off guard by Micah's mouth pressing against hers. Casey put both of her arms around Micah's neck as the kiss deepened. The want to put her hands all over Casey overcame Micah, but she restrained herself. Being a novice at, well, everything, she felt inept.

"Girls!" a voice yelled from the bottom of the stairs. "Dinner!"

Micah pulled away from Casey quickly and they both stood there quietly. Casey smiled.

"Huh. That's a side of you I never thought I'd see. What was that?"

Micah blushed. "I was kissing you back," she said innocently and walked over to the bedroom door. She opened it. "Coming!" she called downstairs.

"Are you?" Casey laughed.

Micah's expression turned horrified, which made Casey laugh harder. "It's time for dinner!" She grabbed Casey's hand and pulled her down the stairs, but let go before they reached the bottom.

Micah and Casey headed into the kitchen. Micah's dad was already sitting at the table and her mom was walking toward him with the pan of macaroni.

"Here it is! Mom's famous mac n' cheese!" Mrs. Williams boasted. Her parents laughed and Micah made a mental note to teach them to be less obvious.

Micah and Casey took their seats next to one another, across from Micah's parents.

Casey took a bite and smiled at Micah's mom. "Wow, this is great." She casually put her other hand on Micah's leg, causing Micah to stiffen. Micah coughed into her napkin the water she had just taken a sip of. She held up her hand.

"I'm alright. No one panic."

Mrs. Williams smiled back at Casey. "I know. It's great, huh?"

"Mom," Micah said, "humility."

Mr. Williams and Casey both laughed a little as they continued eating, and Mrs. Williams grinned at her daughter. "I've earned my bragging rights."

"She sure did," Micah's dad chimed in. Micah gave up and ate her dinner.

"So, Casey, do you take classes with Micah?" Mr. Williams asked between bites of food.

Casey nodded as she finished chewing a mouthful of macaroni. "Yes, we have English class together. That's how we met."

Micah nodded in agreement.

"Do you know Emily?" Mrs. Williams asked.

Casey shrugged. "Sort of."

"Do you have any siblings?"

"Mom, will you just let her eat?"

Casey put her hand on Micah's shoulder for a second. "It's okay." She then looked at Micah's mother.

"Yes. I have a brother, but he lives in California with my mom."

"Oh, so you live here in Boston with just your dad? That's interesting."

"Yeah. My brother comes to visit on the holidays, though, and he and I talk about once a month. He's cool. We're pretty tight."

"It's good to be tight," Mr. Williams commented. Micah looked up at her dad and shook her head in shame.

"Well, I'm getting full," Micah said, putting her hands over her stomach.

Mrs. Williams looked at her daughter's empty plate. "Micah, I told you not to eat too quickly."

"Sorry, Mom."

"I'm pretty full as well," Casey said. "Dinner was great. Thanks so much."

"You're welcome," Mrs. Williams said. "And Micah, you still have dish duty."

"I'm on it." Micah picked up some of the plates. Casey began to help her carry the dinnerware over to the sink.

Micah looked at Casey apologetically. "We don't have a dishwasher."

"It's okay. I know how to use a sponge." She began washing. "Besides, I'm good with my hands." She winked at Micah. Micah shot back a look of panic.

"Stop," she whispered as Casey tried to hold in a laugh. "You keep washing. I'll dry?"

"Deal," Casey agreed and they silently finished cleaning up together.

After the dishes were done and the table was cleaned off, Micah and Casey were excused from the kitchen.

Micah's pulse accelerated as she led Casey upstairs. They entered her bedroom. Casey walked over to Micah's DVD collection as Micah closed the door. Micah got a whiff of the fragrant fabric softener emanating from Casey's blouse. The scent replicated a blend of baby powder and a false sense of chasteness. Micah's temperature soared. Micah opened her mouth to suggest that they watch the movie in the living room, a more wholesome environment, but was too nervous to speak.

"What do you want to watch?" Casey asked without taking her eyes off Micah's expansive movie library.

"You didn't tell me about your brother," Micah said. *Why doesn't anybody tell me anything?*

"You never asked." Casey turned to face Micah. "Actually, you don't ask much about me, now that I think of it."

Micah frowned. "No, I guess not. Sorry about that."

Micah walked over to where Casey stood, glanced at her movies, and then back at Casey. "How about we get to know each other a bit before the movie? You know, like talk for a few minutes?"

Casey sat on Micah's floor with her back against Micah's bed. "Alright. So that's some *Blonde Crusader* poster you've got going on."

Micah sat next to her. "Yeah, I'm a fan of the show."

"You think?" Casey said, laughing.

"Well, yeah, but actually, Emily gave it to me after she forced me to watch the entire series. She's a bigger fan."

Casey nodded. "So you like blonde girls who wear leather and kill vampires?"

Micah smiled. "Something like that." She looked over at Casey. "But I can make exceptions."

Casey smirked. "Are you hitting on me?"

"I'm trying," Micah said shyly. Her focus drifted to the floor. She felt Casey's stare. As Micah summoned the courage to look up, Casey kissed her. This kiss was more aggressive than the one before dinner. Micah's body tingled all over. She ran her hands through Casey's hair, her fingers getting tangled in the loose curls. Casey began progressively moving on top of Micah on the floor. Casey's hands slowly slid across Micah's breasts, still covered by her shirt.

Micah tried to identify the unsettling physical responses, intrigued and overwhelmed by her swelling excitement. She did not trust that she was ready for this. As hard as it was, she slowly eased Casey off her. She ended the kiss with another soft brush against Casey's cheek.

Micah caught her breath and laughed timidly. "Okay, so how about that chat and then a movie?"

Casey put her hand on Micah's knee and ran it up to Micah's thigh, just high enough to make Micah flinch. "You scared?" she asked.

Micah shook her head. "No!" Her confidence was almost believable, save for her voice cracking.

"Why are you scared?" Casey moved her hand off Micah's leg and took Micah's hand. "Micah, I can literally see your muscles tighten up. Relax."

Micah stared at her. What should she say? She could keep kissing Casey, but her parents might come up to the room. Also, she had no idea how to be intimate with a girl. She didn't even have experience being intimate with herself.

"I won't hurt you," Casey whispered.

Micah shook her head but said nothing. Casey sighed.

"Okay, girl, what do you want to know about me?" She squeezed Micah's hand. "Ask me anything."

Micah relaxed for the first time all evening. "Seriously?"

"Sure. Shoot."

"Okay, when did you realize you were gay?"

Casey laughed. "Wow, you don't hold back, do you?"

Micah laughed too, realizing she shared her mother's inability to be subtle.

"I was eleven," Casey answered. "I had the biggest crush on this girl in my math class, Melissa Brown."

"That young? Really?"

"Yes. And yourself?" Casey asked, half teasing and half serious.

"Uh." Micah looked around her room. "So that's all for questions. How about we watch a vintage '80s movie?"

"Answer the question, Micah, or I will tickle the shit out of you and you'll be forced into confession."

"Is that a threat?" Micah asked, wanting Casey to touch her again even if it were just a tickle.

Casey nodded. "Oh, you're asking for it!" Casey knelt in front of Micah. She raised her hands and Micah automatically threw her arms around her own chest, thinking Casey was going to tickle her. Instead, Casey slowly began unbuttoning her own shirt, flaunting a lacey black bra. Micah was speechless. She became insecure about her own basic bra, but mostly she was fascinated that Casey had once again disarmed her.

"We'll watch your '80s movie, but you have to answer the question first. Or I'll do something that will make you squirm more than tickling you ever could. And *that's* a threat." Casey sounded serious. Micah wasn't sure what Casey meant and before she could ask, Casey laughed.

"Eyes up here, Micah."

Micah's cheeks reddened. She had unintentionally been staring at Casey's chest instead of her face. She met Casey's eyes.

"Uh…what? Yes. Sorry."

Casey leaned in closer to Micah. "When did you realize you were gay?"

Micah sucked in as much air as she could and released it in a slow breath. She smiled sheepishly. "Well, I was *going* to say a few weeks before our first kiss when we had just started talking. But if I didn't know then, I *definitely* know now."

Casey laughed and kissed Micah innocently on the cheek. She began buttoning her shirt back up. Micah reached for Casey unconsciously. She stopped herself and was about to put her hand down, but Casey grabbed it gently by the wrist.

"You want to touch me?"

"Your confidence tells me you're really experienced. That's kind of intimidating," Micah replied.

Casey let go of Micah's wrist. "I have a tiny bit of experience. I'm confident because I see it in your eyes that you want me."

Micah swallowed hard. "This is the most intense slumber party I've ever had." They both laughed. "Casey, listen. I need to tell you something, but your exposed skin is distracting."

Casey got off her knees and sat on the floor. She finished buttoning her shirt, looking a little embarrassed since Micah hadn't accepted her invitation. "Tell me what?"

Micah took Casey's hands in hers. "I like you a lot." She thought about what she wanted to say next. "Yes, I'm nervous, of course. And yes, I want to touch you. But I want it to be on my own terms. Does that make sense?"

Casey smiled and looked into Micah's sincere blue eyes. "You're not like anyone I've ever met."

"Sorry," Micah said and started to pull away, but Casey tightened her grip. "Micah, it's a good thing." She leaned over and kissed Micah softly. This kiss was lighter than its predecessor but just as deep. Mouths open. Tongues touching. It lasted for a few minutes until Casey backed away.

"You ready for that movie? I say *Wealthy at Heart*," Casey suggested.

Micah stood up. "Ha! No way! *Detention Time Blues* is way better."

"You don't even let your guests choose the movie? That's kind of rude," Casey teased.

"Oops. Okay, *Wealthy at Heart* sounds good." She took the movie out of its case and put it in the DVD player. Then Micah moved the pillows around on the bed, so that the two of them could lie together and see the TV without a problem. "How's this?" she asked, propping up the last one.

Casey stared at Micah. "Seriously? You want me to watch a movie with you. On your bed."

Micah nodded. "Yes. I trust you." *Do I?*

Casey nodded and held up her hands as if she had been caught doing something illegal. "I'll be good." She lay next to Micah and the movie started. Micah got up and shut off the bedroom lights. She lay back down next to Casey and took her hand.

"Casey?"

"Yes?"

"Why did you stop?"

Casey looked at Micah and smiled. "Micah, you drive me crazy. I'm trying not to come on too strong. Then you'll really run away."

Micah let out a laugh of disbelief. "I drive you crazy? Have you seen *yourself?*"

Casey stopped smiling. "Have you seen *yourself?*"

Before Micah could answer, Casey continued, "Look, you have beautiful blue eyes, a luminous smile, a great personality. If I can gauge correctly, you have a nice body. You know, based on what I can tell, all your layers of clothing aside."

Micah's discomfort reappeared as she did not know how to receive so many compliments at once. "Thanks."

"I'm just saying," Casey said. "Who wouldn't want you?"

The emotional overload subdued Micah and she recoiled slightly. Casey recognized this shift, brushed a few hairs off Micah's face, and kissed her forehead.

"Here it is. My parents got divorced when I was twelve. My mom knew, or at least I think she knew, I was different, and I honestly believe she didn't want to deal with it. She's kind of a religious freak. So my dad kept me and my mom took my brother. She and I don't speak."

Micah looked over and saw in the dark a few tears dripping down Casey's face. Micah wiped them away with the tip of her thumb and put her arms around Casey. They were wrapped in one another as the movie began. The last thing Micah remembered was the opening credits and the smell of Casey's perfume.

Chapter Six

Casey gently rubbed Micah's arm to wake her up. "Micah," she prompted.

"What time is it?" Micah whispered sleepily.

"It's only like ten o'clock. You fell asleep and missed the movie. I didn't want to wake you," Casey explained, "but your phone started going off." Casey handed Micah her phone.

Micah squinted in the dark as she took the phone from Casey. She listened to the voice message.

"Oh my god! I have to go!" Micah jumped out of the bed. She ran for the bedroom light and turned it on.

Casey sat up. "Micah, what's going on?"

Micah opened the door and looked over at Casey. "Emily's in the hospital. I have to go."

Casey got off the bed and walked over to Micah. "What happened?"

"I don't know, but there's a message from her. She needs a ride home so I'm going to get her."

Casey nodded. "Do you mind if I come?"

Micah closed her eyes as if in pain. "I don't know if that's a good idea. I can drop you off at your house on the way. I'm so sorry."

Casey took Micah's hand and kissed it. "It's okay. I understand."

Micah ran down the stairs calling out for her parents. Her mom emerged from their bedroom, frazzled. "Sweetie, what's going on?"

"Mom!" Micah grasped her mom by the shoulders. "Emily called and she needs a ride home from the hospital. I have no idea what happened, but can I borrow the car?"

Mrs. Williams put her hands on Micah's arms at the bends of her elbows. She noticed Casey making her way down the stairs carrying her bag, and then she looked back at her daughter. "Sure, honey, but call me as soon as you can with an update. And *please* be safe."

Micah nodded and motioned for Casey to hurry, then charged past her mother for the keys in the kitchen. The girls made their way to the car and Micah hopped into the driver's seat.

"Casey, I'm really sorry. I just feel like it's weird if you come along."

Casey got in the passenger side and closed the door. Micah backed out of the driveway carefully.

"I get it, Micah. She's your best friend and she barely knows me."

Micah looked over at her. "Rain check?"

Casey smiled. "Rain check."

Micah pulled the car up to Casey's house within minutes and kept the engine running.

"Okay, I'll talk to you later," Micah said hurriedly.

Casey leaned over and kissed Micah lightly on the lips. "Okay. I'll wait up," she said and got out of the car. Micah watched to make sure she made it inside her house, and then sped off to the hospital. She couldn't imagine why Emily would be there.

Luckily, Micah hit all green lights and was at the hospital in moments. She found a parking spot, vaulted out of the car, and ran as fast as she could to the entrance. When she got inside, she rushed to the front desk. The woman sitting behind the desk was on the phone and held up an index finger to Micah to say, "Hold on."

"Thank god I'm not dying," Micah mumbled in frustration. She heard a familiar voice call her name. She turned around and saw Emily walking towards her. Tears stung Micah instantly. Emily's right eye was black and blue and there were stitches across the side of her forehead.

"It's okay, Micah. I'm alright."

Micah wrapped her arms around Emily tightly. "Emily, what the hell happened? Where are your parents?"

Emily shook her head. "I can't tell my parents what happened."

"Are you going to tell me? Em?"

Emily backed away from Micah a little. "Can we go somewhere and talk, or do you need to get home right away?"

Micah became numb. She nodded. "Come with me." She led Emily outside to the garage and into the car.

"Did I wreck your date?" Emily asked, buckling her seatbelt.

Micah shook her head and turned sideways so she could face her friend. She tried hard not to stare at Emily's wounds. "Everything's fine. Don't worry about it." Micah put her hand over Emily's. "What's going on?"

"Before I tell you..." Emily stared straight ahead at some nearby vehicles.

This can't be good.

Emily finally looked at Micah. "You have to promise not to get mad."

Micah's stomach churned. She did not like where this was going. "I don't know if I can make that promise."

The two of them stared at each other. "Micah, you know me better than anyone, but there's something you don't know about me."

"I thought we didn't keep secrets?"

"I know," Emily said. "That's why I'm telling you."

"Are you pregnant?"

Emily smiled a bit, but her lips quivered. "No."

"Will you please say something?"

"Jared did this."

Micah's body went rigid. Her face blackened. She finally found words. "What? Why?"

Emily took a deep breath. "I told him earlier that I didn't want to go out with him…he was upset."

"So he hit you?" Micah exclaimed angrily.

"No, but he *was* mad. He just called me a bitch and walked away."

"And then?"

Emily moved her hand away from Micah's. "And then I went out. I went to Glitter."

"You went clubbing alone?" Micah asked. As she spoke, something occurred to her. "Emily?"

"What?"

"Isn't that a gay club?"

"Uh huh."

Micah cocked her head, trying to put the pieces together. "Why would you go to a gay club and why would you go alone?"

"I wasn't alone." Emily glanced out of the car window again and then back at Micah. "I was with Sam."

"Sam? Who's Sam?"

"Stevenson."

"What? She's gay?" Micah blurted.

"Micah, it's okay," Emily said softly.

"Wait, you guys are friends?"

"We're not exactly friends…"

Micah's mouth dropped open. "Oh my god. Emily, please tell me this isn't going where I think it's going."

"It's going there," Emily said, her eyes apologetic.

The two of them fell quiet again until Emily broke the silence. "We hook up sometimes."

Micah covered her face with her hands and began shaking her head. "No! What?" She looked up, eyes even darker and tears streaming. "How could you keep this from me? I *came out* to you in a panic…SO afraid to be ostracized…and you didn't even tell me? Do you have any idea how alone I've felt?"

Emily went to put her hand on Micah's shoulder, but Micah pulled away. Emily sighed. "I told you that you wouldn't be alone in lesbian land."

Micah glared at Emily. "Not helping."

"Okay, I'm sorry." Emily was at a standstill. "I sleep with girls, that's all."

"That's all? What the fuck?" Micah's profanity caused Emily to jolt. Micah rarely swore without apologizing afterwards.

"I was afraid that if I told you, I would influence you," Emily said.

"Influence me how?"

"Hear me out, Micah. Last summer I was at a party. You were away on your family vacation. Sam was there and she was the only familiar face, so we got to talking. We were kind of drunk, and we...well, you know."

Micah gripped the steering wheel in a fury. "No, Emily, I don't know. I don't understand any of this...it makes NO sense!"

Emily stayed calm. "Okay, let me try again." Micah eased her grip on the wheel, but did not look at Emily. "I did a lot of messed up stuff that summer. You were away and when you came back I didn't tell you, because you're so..."

"So what?" Micah asked.

"You're just...you play by the rules, and I didn't want you to be disappointed in me. Micah, you're my best friend, and I..."

"You what?" Micah asked flatly.

"I care about what you think," Emily said. "Okay, so I told you I slept with someone that summer. Do you remember?"

"Ugh. Yes, that bro dude, Brian, from the vocational school."

"Right, and also Sam. That summer was the first time I ever had sex. With a boy or a girl." Emily looked down at her hands. "And I haven't drunk since, I swear."

Micah shuddered. "Who *are* you? Why should I even believe you?"

"Please let me finish."

"There's more?"

"Micah, it's about more than who I've slept with or who I sleep with. I'm gay, too. I figured it out when I was young. You know I dated a few guys here and there, slept with Brian, et cetera, but nothing ever clicked. I never even heard from Brian again. Sam and I decided to keep our hookups a secret, because I don't want to be in a relationship and neither does she."

"You guys are friends with benefits?" Micah sneered.

"Yes, something like that. It's just easier."

"How is that easy? And why don't I know any of this?"

"It's easy because my heart belongs to someone else," Emily explained.

"I don't need to know any more. Emily, I can't." Micah wiped away some stray tears with her sleeve.

"Okay, but can I just say a little more?" There was a hint of desperation in Emily's voice.

"Fine. Then I'm taking you home."

"That's fine." Emily stayed focused on Micah, even though Micah still wouldn't look at her. "I kind of thought you were into girls since we were like fourteen. You had a serious crush on what's-her-face from the Smoothie Palace, like borderline obsession. I haven't seen you drink a smoothie since the day you found out she quit." Emily let out a harmless laugh. "And I've been curious about girls ever since I can remember."

Emily stopped talking to give Micah a minute to digest all of this. "When we were younger I didn't say anything, because I felt so abnormal. I didn't know what the feelings were. As we got older, I put it together. And then I still didn't tell you, because I thought you should figure out your sexuality on your own. I didn't want to put ideas in your head or weird you out. I was trying to be a good friend."

"Who else knows?" Micah asked.

"Sam and I are pretty quiet about it. We hit up a club once in awhile and then just…um, hang out after."

Micah was paralyzed. "I feel sick."

"Micah…"

"If you thought I was gay, it would've been helpful if you told me. But you didn't. You let me suffer, because it was so important to *you* that I figure out my sexuality on my own. What about what's important to *me*? And then, here's the kicker. When I told you that I was gay, you *still* didn't tell me the truth about yourself! Why?" Micah erupted.

"You're right. I'm sorry," Emily murmured. "Anyways it doesn't matter. What's done is done."

"Yeah, it's done alright."

"Can I tell you the rest? Because I *do* want you to know," Emily pleaded.

"Do what you want. You seem to be on a roll," Micah retorted.

Emily sighed. "When I found out you had plans with Casey tonight, I made plans with Sam. As we were walking into the club, she held my hand. Jared and his friends were coming from the opposite direction."

Micah finally looked over at Emily, scared for what she was going to hear next.

"He called us dykes, he called me a whore, and he said he understood why I turned him down...because I'm into pussy." Emily stopped, inhaled, and continued, "He pushed Sam away from me and when I went to defend her, he hit me. It was kind of like a really powerful smack in the face. I lost my balance and fell and whacked my head on the curb. Jared and his friends ran away. I had Sam leave me at the hospital alone. That's what happened." A tear escaped from Emily's bruised eye. Micah saw it and fought the urge to comfort her friend.

"Emily, we should go to the police."

"No! No, we shouldn't! Micah, if this gets out, my parents will kill me and they won't understand. Let me deal with this."

"Right, because you're so good at dealing with stuff," Micah said with harsh sarcasm. "Whatever. I don't know how else to help you. I'm taking you home."

"Micah, please. Don't do this."

"Do what? What am I doing? I never lied to you or made you believe I'm someone I'm not. You call yourself a friend? You think you were doing me a favor? Fuck you." Micah fumed.

Emily started to cry.

"Em, I'm sorry I swore at you. I just don't know what's happening. It's like you're a stranger."

"Micah," Emily sobbed.

"What?"

"Please don't tell."

Micah turned the ignition. "I won't," she said dryly and began driving Emily home.

The entire ride was silent. When they finally pulled up to Emily's house, Micah cut the engine. "What are you going to tell your parents?" she asked.

"That I got in a fight with a girl from school." Emily clearly had given this some thought.

"Okay, then that's what I'll tell mine if they ask."

Emily went to hug Micah, but Micah put her hand up to block her. "Don't touch me."

Emily withdrew. "Thank you…for the ride and stuff."

Emily got out of the car, but before closing the door, she poked her head inside. Micah's heart broke at the sight of her bruised face.

"I really am sorry." Emily closed the door and walked up to her house. Micah watched Emily disappear inside and then she heard Emily's parents shouting. Micah sat there and cried.

After a few minutes, she pulled herself together, picked up her phone, and dialed Casey's number.

"Hello?" Casey sounded wide awake.

"Sorry to call so late," Micah said.

"You okay? How's Emily?"

"We're fine. Can I come over?"

There was a stretch of silence on the other end of the phone. "Micah, it's like midnight."

"I'm using the rain check."

"Okay. Text me when you get here and I'll meet you at the back door."

"Thanks," Micah said and hung up. Then she dialed her home phone number. Her mother, on the brink of hysterics, answered on the first ring.

"Micah! Are you okay? Is Emily okay?" her mom screeched into the phone.

"Yeah, Mom. Em got in a fight with some girl from school and her parents weren't around to pick her up from the hospital. She's all alone. Is it okay if I hold onto the car and spend the night? I don't want to leave her." *What's one more lie?*

"Sure, sweetie. Have the car back by nine tomorrow morning. Your dad and I have errands to run."

"Okay, thanks."

"Micah, call if you need anything."

"I will. Goodnight, Mom," Micah said and hung up. She turned off the phone and then headed over to Casey's house. *Play by the rules, my ass!*

Chapter Seven

Micah pulled the car up to Casey's house. Before getting out, she checked her reflection in the rearview mirror. She ignored the empty eyes that stared back and wiped the remaining tears off her face. Her feet felt steady on the pavement as she exited the car. She marched to the back of Casey's house and texted her that she had arrived. A few seconds later, the porch light went on and Casey opened the door.

"Hey. Coming in?" Casey asked. She hadn't changed out of her clothes from earlier.

Micah nodded as Casey took her hand and brought her inside the unlit kitchen. "My dad's here, but he's asleep on the sofa." Micah could hear that the TV was on in the next room. Casey led her over to a door that looked like it went to the basement.

"Where are we going?" Micah asked.

Casey smiled. "My room."

Micah knit her brows airily in response, then trailed behind Casey down some stairs. She couldn't believe she was in Casey's bedroom. Casey sat on the bed and motioned for Micah to sit next to her, which she did.

"You're still dressed," Micah pointed out.

"Yes, I typically don't answer the door naked," Casey said with a laugh. "I was waiting up for you, watching reruns of crime shows."

Micah did not react.

Casey's forehead scrunched. "What's going on? Have you been crying?"

With resolve, Micah cupped the side of Casey's face and drew Casey in for a kiss. As the kiss came to a slow ending, Casey pulled Micah closer for more. Micah allowed herself to get lost in the soft touch of Casey's lips against her own. She started unbuttoning Casey's shirt. Casey stopped her.

"Wait," Casey said breathlessly. "There's no pressure. You know I want you, but there's no need to rush."

Micah lay back on Casey's bed and stared up at the ceiling. Casey turned her gaze downward and studied the outline of Micah's face. Micah took hold of Casey's hand and coaxed Casey on top of her.

"I don't want to wait," Micah whispered.

Casey began kissing Micah again, but hesitated while undressing her. "Are you sure?" Casey asked.

Micah silenced Casey with another kiss. She became very aware of the weight of Casey's body on top of her own. Casey's hands explored her with a natural certainty that Micah attempted to imitate. For the rest of the night, she was able to escape the pain of betrayal inside of her.

Micah tried to open her eyes as the sunlight peeked through Casey's bedroom window. Casey was looking at her, smiling.

"Hi, sleepy," she said and kissed Micah's bare shoulder. Micah realized that neither of them had on any clothes under the sheets. Last night's events blurred through her mind.

"Were you watching me sleep? How long have you been awake? What time is it?" Micah asked.

Casey leaned over and kissed Micah lightly on the lips. "Do you always have so many questions when you wake up?"

Micah furrowed her brow.

"It's eight o'clock, I've been up for about ten minutes, and yes, I was watching you sleep. You're cute when you drool," Casey said.

Micah's hand flew to her mouth to wipe away anything that might be there. Casey was laughing and shaking her head.

"I'm teasing. Are you okay?" Casey asked.

Micah wasn't sure what this question was pertaining to. "Why? Are you okay?"

Casey's grin widened. "Um, yeah. I'm fantastic." Her eyes sparkled at Micah. "You're a pro. You sure you never did that before?"

Micah's cheeks grew hot. "Don't say that. It's embarrassing."

Casey wrapped her legs around Micah's. "Why? You should be proud of that."

Micah shook her head. "No more. Stop talking about it," she pleaded.

"Oh. Okay?" She disentangled her legs from Micah's. "Are you having regrets?"

"No," Micah responded immediately. "No, I didn't mean for it to sound like that. I…I'm just uncomfortable."

"Micah, you shouldn't be having sex if you can't even talk about it," Casey said.

Micah looked up at the door leading to the kitchen. "Oh my god! Do you think your dad heard us?"

Casey laughed. "Nah, he could sleep through the apocalypse."

The strain in Micah's face relaxed slightly. "Right. Okay. Um, well, I need to get going. I told my mom I'd have the car home by nine."

Casey sulked. "What's happening? You seem really off."

Micah shrugged. "No, I'm just tired. I'm going to take a nap when I get home."

"Okay," Casey said skeptically. She got out of the bed and walked around the room completely disrobed. Casey picked up articles of Micah's outfit from yesterday and tossed them over to her. "Here you go. I'm guessing you feel awkward being naked and all."

Micah hugged the clothes close to her. "Thanks."

"I've seen all of you. You've got nothing to be ashamed of."

"Uh, thanks?" Micah said. "You either."

Casey shook her head. "You're quite the smooth talker."

She watched Micah begin to dress. Micah was struggling to hook her bra; Casey sat behind Micah on the bed and clasped the bra for her. Then she kissed the small of her back, which sent shivers down Micah's body.

"Casey, look, I don't regret anything." Micah got up and finished getting dressed. "I kind of can't believe that actually happened, because we're not even…"

Casey waited as Micah struggled to speak. She took Micah's hand. "Going steady?" she proposed with a smile.

Micah smiled back, sick to her stomach again. "I should go." She glanced over at the alarm clock on Casey's nightstand. "Thanks for letting me stay the night."

"You're welcome, but the pleasure was truly mine," Casey said.

Micah's shoulders raised. "If you say so." She started towards the staircase and turned to look at Casey again. "Casey?"

"Yes, my lover?" Casey said playfully.

Micah pointed her finger at Casey. "No."

Casey stopped laughing. "Yes, Micah, you were saying?"

"My mom's dinner was from a box."

Casey smiled. "I know. I live off that stuff. It's okay."

"Cool, just wanted to put the truth out there. I'll talk to you soon."

Casey stood up from the bed and to Micah's relief, pulled the comforter around herself. "Can I walk you out?"

"That's okay," Micah said and kissed Casey on the cheek. Micah slinked up the stairs and out of Casey's house.

Micah got in the car and wept as she drove home. She had promised herself that she would never sleep with anyone she wasn't dating. She didn't want to be like Emily, living a life full of "hooking up." *What did I just do?* Micah questioned. Then it occurred to her that she had done something reckless unbeknownst to Emily; *this* idea invoked a warped pride within her.

By the time she arrived at her house, it was 8:55 and she had stopped crying. She fumbled for her keys and slowly made her way inside. Mr. and Mrs. Williams were sitting at the kitchen table.

"Oh, hey, guys."

"Where were you last night?" her mom asked angrily. Micah looked at her dad, who stared into his coffee cup.

"What? At Em's, remember?" Micah wavered.

Micah's mom got up from her chair. "Funny, because shortly after you called to ask if you could stay at Emily's house, Emily showed up here. It was about, oh, a little after midnight. She was looking for you. I called you *several* times and your phone kept going to voicemail."

Micah's heart sank. She lowered her head. "Mom, it's a long story."

Mrs. Williams stood in front of her. "Look at me, young lady."

Micah met her mother's eyes. "Get upstairs and clean up. We're going to talk later, and you are going to tell me the truth if you can remember what that is."

Micah sagged and shuffled upstairs. She couldn't recollect the last time her mom sounded this upset, and she didn't want "later" to arrive.

She opened the door to her bedroom and froze. Emily was sitting on her bed. The covers were rustled and she discerned that Emily had spent the night. The girls stared at each other and then heard the sound of a throat clearing behind Micah. Micah pivoted to see her mom.

"You two are best friends. Work it out and get your stories straight before I kick both of your asses," she said and slammed the door shut.

Micah then slowly turned to face Emily. "I have nothing to say to you."

Emily stood up. "I'm sorry. I had nowhere else to go last night. After my parents were done reaming me out, they started yelling at each other. I couldn't stand it so I left. I came here, because"—Emily looked around Micah's bedroom—"I always come here."

"Get out," Micah said firmly, stifling tears.

"Where were you? I was worried. You never stay out all night."

Micah moved away from the door so that she wasn't blocking Emily's exit path. "Emily, leave."

Emily's chest heaved. "You're missing one of the earrings from your left ear," she said softly and walked out. Micah touched her left ear and felt the empty space where her third hoop ordinarily was.

"Great. That's just great," she mumbled to herself.

Chapter Eight

Micah showered and curled up on her bed, her wet hair soaking through the pillowcase. She could smell a mixture of perfumes lying there: Casey's and Emily's.

She looked up at her desk where there was a framed picture of her and Emily from earlier that year. They stood outside of The Bean, arms around each other, holding up their lattes.

She remembered that that was when Emily began to refer to the attractive barista who worked there as "Hot Megan." Micah shook her head. *How did I not know?* She was about to reach deeper into the pockets of her memory to see if she could conjure up any more similar instances. Just then, her mom walked in and Micah sat up, holding on tightly to her pillow.

Mrs. Williams took Micah's desk chair and dragged it over to the bed. She sat on it, quietly staring down at Micah. "Micah, please tell me what's going on."

Micah lowered her head. "Mom, I'm sorry."

"About what? What did you do?"

Micah ran her hand over her face. "It's not about what I did. Well, not really. It's about who I *am*," Micah growled as the waterworks began.

Mrs. Williams moved from the chair to the bed and put her arm around Micah. "Honey, I can't help you unless you tell me what's going on."

"Mom, I"—Micah looked into her mother's worried eyes—"I lied to you." There was a stretch of silence and Micah shriveled inside.

Her mother exhaled, then spoke. "You are my child, Micah. I know you lied to me. I want to hear the truth now."

Micah dropped her head again. "Mom, I'm kind of…ugh, why is this so hard?" She looked over once more at the picture of her and Emily and then at her mom. "You were right. I do like girls…I think I'm gay."

Mrs. Williams cradled her daughter. "I know. I've always known."

Micah pulled away. "What? What do you mean you've always known? How come I didn't know?"

Her mother smiled. "I know you. I've been observing you for your entire life. I had a feeling and I figured you would eventually realize on your own. It wasn't my place to tell you."

"Why am I last to know that I'm gay? First Emily, now you?"

Her mother sighed. "Is this why you and Emily are fighting?"

Micah sat very still. "Kind of. I got mad that Emily also knew I was gay and failed to tell me." *Okay, so a half-truth is better than a full out lie*, Micah convinced herself.

"So you two had this fight last night?" her mother asked. "Did you give her that shiner?"

Micah laughed a little. "No, I would never hurt Emily. We had an argument, and then I went to Casey's. I kind of spent the night there."

More silence filled the room. "So you are gay with Casey and not with Emily?"

Micah buried her face in the pillow and muffled a simple, "Yes."

Her mom gave her another squeeze and stood up. Micah watched to see what was going to happen.

"Your father and I love you. We don't care that you're gay. We do care about your safety. When you take the car and lie about where you are and where you're going and who you're going to be with, well, that is what infuriates us. When Emily showed up here looking like she did, I didn't know what to think. But I certainly wasn't going to send her back to the hell hole she calls home. She's like family." Micah's mom stopped to think for a moment. "I'm sure Emily meant no harm when she didn't tell you that she thought you were gay, the same way that I meant no harm. It's part of your journey. There are some things you need to figure out alone, but you don't necessarily have to *be* alone. Does that make sense?"

Micah nodded. "Yes."

"Talk to Emily. And as for your lying about where you were – two weeks without socialization. You go to school and you come home. And any girl that you are more than friends with cannot sleep over. I wasn't born yesterday. I know you're going to do what you're going to do, just not under this roof. Okay?"

"Okay," Micah said softly.

Mrs. Williams bestowed another stern smile on Micah, then put the chair back in its place. She turned around. "That Casey girl…"

Micah looked up. "What about her?"

"Does she make you happy?"

Micah nodded. "Yeah." As she answered this question, she realized that she hadn't spent enough time with Casey to be sure. Casey made her excited and she enjoyed being around her. Did that define "making someone happy"?

"Okay, good," her mother said and walked away, closing the door behind her.

Micah laid down on her bed and let out a sigh of relief. She did it! She had come out to her mom. She grabbed her phone, immediately went to text Emily, and then stopped herself. She put the phone down, rolled onto her side, and brought her knees back up to her chest. At some point, she must have fallen asleep.

She woke up to the sound of silverware clinking. The room was dark; her parents must be setting the dinner table. She looked at her phone. The last time she checked it was noon and now the time read 6:58 p.m. She had slept for seven hours! She saw that she had two missed calls: one from Emily and one from Casey. They both left messages. Hesitantly, Micah listened to them.

The first was from Casey: "Hey, you. Just calling to see how things went when you got home. What are you up to? Give me a call back and let me know you're okay. I, uh, I had a really great night last night. Okay, bye," and Casey hung up. Micah stared at her phone. She contemplated erasing the message, but decided to keep it.

She then listened to Emily's: "Micah, hi. Look, I know you're mad at me and that's fine, but I really would like to talk to you so we can sort this out. You're my best friend and things don't feel right when you and I aren't speaking. I don't ever remember us *not* speaking. Please, Micah, I need to talk to you, because I—" The phone cut off Emily's voice, probably because her message was long. Why didn't Emily call again to finish it? And what was the end of that sentence going to be? She considered calling Emily back, but then changed her mind. She pressed "delete" and hung up the phone. She got up and made her way downstairs.

Her parents had dinner ready. "Micah, care to join us?" her dad said, motioning to the seat at the table that Micah usually took.

"Sure. Thanks, Dad," Micah said as she sat down.

"Your mom told me about your little chat earlier," her dad continued.

Micah glanced at her mother and then faced her dad. "Oh really?"

"Micah, honey, I love you. No more lies, okay?" her dad said, half-smiling.

"Okay, Dad," Micah agreed.

Since she was being quarantined, Micah decided to have her own movie marathon after dinner. She skimmed through her collection and picked out a classic. She had just gotten comfortable on her bed when her phone rang. She looked at the number. It was Casey.

"Hello?" Micah answered.

"Hey, Micah. Thanks for calling me back to let me know all is well."

"I'm sorry."

"Micah, you may or may not believe this, but I care about you," Casey confessed.

Micah smiled. "I appreciate that."

"Is everything okay?"

"Yeah, everything's okay, but I'm kind of grounded for lying to my parents so I could spend last night with you," Micah explained.

"Ah, I see. Are you cleared to use your phone?"

"I think so. My mom would've taken it from me if it were off limits."

"Well, I guess we'll just have to have a conversation on the phone then." Casey's tone was optimistic.

"I feel bad," Micah divulged.

"About what?" Casey asked.

"Last night."

"Shit, Micah. Are you serious? You regret it? I can't play these games."

"I'm not playing games. I feel like we went from hanging out to having sex without all of the steps in between," Micah said softly. "That's not exactly how I wanted it to be for us, but I…I let it happen. In the moment I wanted it to happen."

"I feel the same way and I feel responsible for that," Casey said.

"Why?" Micah asked, touched by Casey's sincerity.

"Because I'm a little more, um, seasoned, than you from what I understand. I feel like I should've taken things more slowly with you. But I wanted you so bad and I got greedy. I'm sorry."

Micah wasn't sure what to say in response. How was Casey so comfortable discussing sexual desires? "I have a mind of my own. I'm responsible for my choices and I like you and I…" Micah's thoughts raced with images of Casey's naked body on top of her own.

"Hello? You there?" Casey asked.

"Here, yup."

Casey laughed. "Wow. You're an easy read even over the phone. I understand if you're not comfortable talking about this, but eventually we'll have to."

"Why? Why do we have to analyze this?" Micah asked.

"Because something happened between us last night and I would like for it to happen again, but differently," Casey explained. "Can we start over?"

"I'm not sure I follow," Micah admitted.

"Like, let's finish where we left off Friday night before the movie. The whole getting-to-know-you thing. Is that okay?" Casey spoke softly.

"Sure."

"What's your favorite color?" Casey asked.

"This is so random," Micah said, rolling her eyes.

"Just humor me and answer the question."

"Black."

"That's dismal," Casey said, laughing.

"It goes with everything," Micah rebutted.

"Not true. It clashes with brown."

Micah had to agree. "Okay, okay. What's your favorite color?"

"Any variation of blue. I'm not that picky," Casey said. "Now what do you like to do when you want to be alone with your thoughts?"

"I'm currently afraid of all of my thoughts," Micah responded.

"Answer, please."

"I don't know. Listen to music, I guess. You?" Micah asked back.

"Good choice. I like to sit in the dark with candles."

"And you're calling me morbid?"

Casey laughed. "No. It's like meditating. It's really powerful." Casey let the quiet sit between them for a moment, and then continued, "We should try it together sometime. I can show you."

"I suppose we could. You don't strike me as someone who would be into all that New Age hype," Micah said.

"There's a lot you don't know about me. That's why we're doing this. Would you like to know more?"

A smile played across Micah's face. "Maybe."

"Excellent. Well, we'll save some for later. I'm gonna let you enjoy *She's Nowhere*."

Micah looked around her, alarmed. "Um, how do you know what movie I'm watching?"

"I can hear the music in the background. I'm a soundtrack genius," Casey gloated.

"Cool! I look forward to hearing more about that special skill." Micah immediately wished she had chosen her words more carefully.

"Good, because I have a few more special skills I can demonstrate for you." Casey laughed.

There was another brief silence.

"You blushing?" Casey asked.

"Yes," Micah conceded.

"Nice. Sweet dreams, Micah."

"Goodnight, Casey," Micah said and they both hung up the phone. She sighed. *Alright. We agreed that we moved a little too fast. This is a good thing.* She looked at the time to see that it was only nine o' clock. Her eyelids were laboring to stay open. She sluggishly went to restart the movie.

"Micah! Can you come down here?" her mom called up to her.

"Ugh!" Micah paused the DVD and headed downstairs. She stopped abruptly when she saw Emily standing at the door.

"Hey, buddy," Emily said with a small wave.

Mrs. Williams looked at Micah. "You have ten minutes. Then your grounding will resume." She walked away to give the girls some privacy.

"Why are you here, Emily?" Micah asked. "You don't give up, do you?"

"I wanted to see you. You didn't call me back. I called earlier and left you a message. And no, I don't give up. Not on my friends."

"I got your message. I didn't call you back. Clearly you didn't get *that* message," Micah hissed, stunned by her own cruelty.

Emily shoved her hands deep into her jean pockets, fighting back tears.

"So, you're grounded?" Emily tried to steady her voice.

"Yup," Micah said, stone-faced.

"That sucks," Emily said.

Micah looked behind her to make sure her mom was still gone, and then spun back to Emily. "I don't want to see you and I don't know why you don't understand that."

"What? Are you going to hate me forever?" Emily asked. "You're mad at me because I had a secret? Is that it? And let me guess. You're completely flawless and have no secrets, right?"

"Yes!" Micah nodded emphatically. "Yes, that is exactly why I'm upset. You were like living a double life AND you didn't even support me in coming out. I would've felt a lot better knowing my best friend was into girls, too. But noooooo, you kept that from me!" Micah recalled her night with Casey. Maybe she shouldn't be laying into Emily so hard.

Emily bit her bottom lip and shook her head. "You don't get it."

"Get what?" Micah snapped.

"Forget it. Look, I apologize and I'm asking you to forgive me."

"Goodnight, Emily," Micah said and began leading Emily to the door.

Emily stood there, looking sadly at Micah. "Good night. You know how to reach me if you decide you want to be friends again."

Micah watched Emily turn away and walk slowly down the street. She waited until she could no longer see Emily, and then she stepped inside the house and closed the door. She wheeled around and her mom was there, shaking her head, arms crossed over her chest.

"What?" Micah asked defensively.

"Just remember, someday you might be asking for forgiveness. And if that day were to come, you would want it, wouldn't you?" her mother asked.

"Were you eavesdropping on me?" Micah accused.

Micah's mom pointed to the stairway, signaling for Micah to go to her room. Micah stomped up the stairs. Her mother had just given her way too much to think about.

Chapter Nine

Micah's alarm prompted her to get ready for school on Monday morning. She groaned and eased herself out of bed. She had spent her entire Sunday without talking to anyone. Instead, she had buried herself in homework and chores. Casey had given her space and Emily must have finally accepted that Micah needed to process everything from Friday night. Now it was time to return to school and face reality. She showered, dressed, and headed downstairs.

Mrs. Williams was sitting at the table with coffee and the paper when Micah entered the kitchen.

"Good morning. Your father already left, but he told me to tell you to go into school today and be 'loud and proud.'"

Micah and her mother both rolled their eyes and chuckled. Micah microwaved some instant oatmeal and sat down. She had a few minutes before she had to leave to catch the bus.

"How did you sleep?" her mother asked.

"Okay. You?"

"Alright. Micah, I'm concerned. I know your dad is trying to be supportive and so am I, but I don't know if it's wise to let everyone know about your…gayness."

Micah stopped eating and looked at her mom. "My gayness? Try again, Mom."

"Well, you know what I mean." Her mother fiddled with the paper. "And besides, you and Emily aren't talking, so I don't know who will be there for you at school."

"Mom, please. I don't need a bodyguard."

"I know that, Micah. I'm just worried."

Micah got up and put her bowl in the sink. "I get it, Mom. I'm a little worried too, but this is life." Micah put her books in her bag. "Okay, I gotta go. I'll be home after school as planned."

Her mom nodded. "Give me a kiss goodbye."

Micah leaned over, gave her mom a hug, and kissed her on the cheek. "Bye," she said quickly and left the house.

The bus was late. She got on and sat amongst the strangers she saw every morning. She was thankful that she took a public bus and not a rumor-filled school bus. Micah thought of Emily and cringed. Jared was popular so his Friday nights were probably of great interest to many of her classmates. Emily's eye was most likely still bruised and it was clear she had gotten stitches. People were going to be asking her a million questions. How would she handle it? Would Emily turn to Sam for support? Should Micah offer support? Micah shook her head and mumbled, "No," not realizing she had said it aloud. The woman across from her looked up and Micah averted her eyes. Before Micah could configure a plan, they arrived at school. Reluctantly, Micah got off the bus. She had no idea what she was walking into.

Micah approached her locker. It was absurd, but she was surprised that Emily wasn't there. She hurried to homeroom and took her seat.

Moments later, Emily appeared in the doorway, holding out a folded note. Micah instinctively went over to retrieve it. She was right – Emily did not look much better. They stared at one another for what seemed like forever, then Micah accepted the piece of paper. She put it in her pocket and watched Emily walk away.

En route back to her chair, Micah passed a small cluster of boys laughing in the middle of the room. She overheard Jared saying Emily's name, followed by "gave it up" and "showed her who's boss." Micah, operating on autopilot, walked over to Jared and his group of friends. They stopped laughing and looked up.

Jared raised his eyebrow. "Um, can I help you?" he asked pompously.

Micah stood there. "I heard what you just said. That's my friend you're talking about and I don't appreciate you telling lies. Why don't you tell your buddies what a fucking bully you are?"

Jared stood up, towering over Micah. Micah continued, "I thought you were a good guy."

Jared laughed and so did the kids around him. "You thought wrong, bitch." He looked at his friends, who all kept laughing. "And your friend there, well, she liked it. A lot."

Micah couldn't help herself. She threw the hardest punch she could muster right in the center of his face. For a few seconds, everything around her went white from the pain shooting up her arm. But then she saw red: the blood coming from Jared's nose.

The homeroom teacher walked in screaming as everyone in the class reacted. Half of the students were silent in shock and the other half clamored for a fight.

"Shit! Fucking bitch broke my nose!" Jared howled.

The teacher led Micah out of the room as he ordered another student to take Jared to the nurse's office. Micah attempted to pull away from the teacher, still yelling at Jared.

"Why don't you hit me back? You're not above hitting girls, I hear? So let's see it!"

"Micah!" the teacher scolded. He yanked her into the hallway where the students from the next homeroom over, including Emily, were already emerging. They all witnessed the spectacle of Jared's blood splattered across the front of his shirt and soaking through the paper towels held to his face. The teacher escorted Micah down the corridor. Emily impulsively followed them to the principal's office.

A few whispers could be heard, but mostly the kids were confused. Micah was a peacekeeper who got along with almost everyone. Jared was popular and rarely got in trouble. Only the fact that Emily had chased after Micah was no mystery.

Micah sat in the waiting area of the principal's office while he phoned her parents. She could only imagine what kind of trouble she was going to be in now. She held an ice pack around her right hand, which pulsed painfully. She leaned back to wallow and saw Emily standing there.

"What? Do you lurk in doorways now like a friggin' vampire?" Micah asked harshly. Emily moved inside the room and opened her mouth to say something. Just then, Casey came running in, went straight for Micah, and wrapped her arms around her.

"Micah, my god! Are you okay?" Casey asked, scrutinizing the ice pack.

"How did you know I was here?"

"After the bell rang for first period, I came to find you to give you this." Casey opened her palm, revealing Micah's missing earring. In the distance, Emily took a step back. Casey continued, "When you weren't there, I asked your homeroom teacher if you were absent. He told me you were here but didn't say why. Why *are* you here? Did someone try to hurt you?" Casey leapt up, fists formed in preparation for a fight.

Micah held up her functioning hand. "Casey, it's okay. I'm okay." She took a deep breath. "It's a long story."

Casey sat back down and uncovered the earring for a second time. "Want me to?" she asked, offering to put the ring back in Micah's ear. Micah wouldn't be able to hook the hoop singlehandedly so she nodded in compliance. As Casey finished putting the earring back in its rightful place, Emily cleared her throat to remind the two girls that they were not alone in the room.

"Oh. Hi, Emily," Casey said.

"Casey," Emily acknowledged, and then inched closer.

"Micah, why did you do that?" Emily asked.

Casey's eyes passed between Emily and Micah. "What did you do?" Casey asked.

Emily stared at Casey. "Jared was being a dick so she hit him," she explained.

Casey reevaluated Micah's hand. "You *hit* him? Why? What did he do?"

Emily began to speak again. "He was mouthing off about his imaginary sexual conquests and my name came up and Micah—"

Casey put both of her hands in the air. "Whoa, whoa, wait a second." She looked at Emily's battered face. "Did Jared do that to you?" Casey asked, pointing to Emily's stitches.

Micah closed her eyes and shook her head.

Emily concentrated on Micah and completely ignored Casey's question. "Thank you, but I can take care of myself." Emily retreated, leaving Micah to seek solace in Casey through this very bizarre moment.

"Please tell me what is going on," Casey said.

Micah opened her eyes and said softly, "That's what happened. Jared was spreading rumors so I hit him."

"That's all you're going to tell me, isn't it?"

Micah nodded.

Casey stared at the pictures on the wall. They were mostly black and white photos of the school and its students over the years. She finally looked at Micah.

"Can you meet me in the girls' locker room during lunch?" Casey asked.

"If my mom doesn't take me home and if I'm not suspended, then yes, I will be there."

Casey lingered in the entranceway, looked around the room again, then settled her gaze on Micah. "Well, I hope to see you there. Good luck, Rocky," she said, smiling slightly on her way out.

Micah sighed. She reached into her jeans and unfolded the note that Emily had given her this morning. It read, "Please meet me after school in the library. I'll be waiting for you." Micah crumpled up the paper and shoved it back into her pocket.

The principal stepped out of his office. "Micah."

"Yes, Mr. Lewis?"

"I have your mother on the phone. In here now."

Micah went into his office and watched the door close behind them. She took a seat across from his desk and he handed her the phone receiver.

"Hi, Mom," Micah said, barely above a whisper.

"Micah, what the hell is going on? You punched a boy in the face?" *She sounds concerned. Better than angry. I'll take it.*

"Mom, can I please explain?"

"I'm waiting."

"There's this kid in my homeroom and he was saying some mean stuff about a girl I know. Like really bad stuff, Ma. And it was all lies and everyone was laughing and I just couldn't stand there and listen." Micah grew fearful of her mother's reaction.

"So you hit him? Is that how your father and I raised you? To hit people when you think they're being mean?" Her mother's tone reached a much higher pitch. *Aaand she's mad.*

"Mom, I think he was talking about me." Micah had to lie to protect Emily. She had no choice.

Her mom took in a sharp breath. "What?"

"Listen, Mom. It's high school and people thrive off talking about each other. And I told you that I can look after myself."

"Are you okay?" Her mother's voice was steadying.

"Yes. My hand hurts, but I'm okay," Micah said, catching a glimpse of Mr. Lewis glaring at her.

"Do you want me to come get you?" her mother asked.

"Mom, I can't miss all my classes. I don't want to fall behind."

"Okay, I'll see you at home. We'll talk more then. I love you. No more fights. Micah, you're a smart girl. Use your words," her mom said and hung up the phone.

Micah handed the receiver to Mr. Lewis. "She said I could stay. Am I going to be suspended?"

Mr. Lewis shook his head. "No. Your mother and I already spoke before I called you in here. When I told her that you had punched a fellow student, she said that she was afraid this 'kind of thing' might happen."

Micah rubbed her forehead with her left hand while he continued.

"She told me that you had recently come out to her and that you were afraid of what people might say. Micah, did Jared say something about you?" Mr. Lewis looked at her sympathetically.

Her mother outed her to the principal! Micah refused to closet herself and make her mother look like a liar. Nor was she willing to break her promise to Emily. If it were discovered that Jared had hit Emily, the cops would most likely get involved. The fallout at Emily's house would be terrible as well. She concluded that the mess would go away fastest if Jared were only guilty of name-calling. *Here come more lies*, Micah thought to herself.

"Yes, Mr. Lewis. I heard Jared telling his friends that I was a dyke."

Disappointment cast over Mr. Lewis's face. "Micah, you know we pride ourselves on being a zero tolerance school?"

"Yes, sir."

He picked up his phone and after a few seconds, Micah heard him say, "After he's done, can you send him up here?" He waited a minute and then hung up the phone. He looked back at Micah.

"Micah, normally, hitting another student calls for suspension. But because you felt threatened and are clearly going through a difficult life transition, I'm going to let this go. You're very lucky that you have a stellar record at this school. This better be the last time I ever see you in here. Understood?"

"Understood," Micah said appreciatively.

"Do you want to talk to the guidance counselor?" he asked, almost as if telling her she had to.

"Not really."

"Well, think about it. I highly encourage you to do so."

Someone knocked on the office door.

"Come in," Mr. Lewis said loudly.

Jared walked in, a bulky bandage over his nose. He scowled at Micah, who grew anxious.

Mr. Lewis pointed to the empty seat next to Micah. "Have a seat, young man," he ordered Jared. Jared hesitated but sat down.

He looked at Mr. Lewis. "What?"

Mr. Lewis stared at the two of them. "Micah tells me that you called her an unacceptable word in homeroom. She was very offended and reacted irrationally. Is this true?" he questioned Jared.

Jared eyeballed Micah with a surprised expression. "That's what you told him?"

Micah glared back. "Don't you ever call me a dyke again."

There was a look of recognition on Jared's face. He replied to Mr. Lewis, "Yes, sir, that's what happened." He shifted to Micah. "Micah, I'm sorry I said that."

Micah nodded. "I'm sorry I broke your nose."

He chuckled. "It's not broken. It was just hit hard."

Mr. Lewis stood up. "Alright. Jared, you know how I feel about bullying."

"Yes, Mr. Lewis."

"Next time I will require you to take the zero tolerance seminar," Mr. Lewis said.

"But we have that at the beginning of every year! I've already sat through it like a thousand times," Jared whined.

"Mmm, I see. So you've attended this school for a thousand years, is that it?" Mr. Lewis asked.

"No," Jared said, looking down.

"Clearly, you weren't paying attention. If anything like this should happen again, you will sit through that seminar until you can recite it verbatim. Are we clear?"

"Yes, sir," Jared answered.

"Are you getting picked up?" Mr. Lewis asked Jared, gesturing to Jared's nose.

"No. I have to be at practice after school or coach will bench me," he explained.

Mr. Lewis nodded. "Fine then. It's settled. Now the two of you get to class."

They both stood up and walked back into the waiting area, heading for the exit. As they entered the hallway, Micah took a left to go to class. Jared started towards the right but stopped.

"Hey, Williams," Jared called to Micah by her last name.

Micah turned to face him. "What?"

"Thanks for not ratting me out. But why didn't you?" he asked suspiciously.

Micah walked over to him and pointed her index finger in his face. "If you touch her again or if you breathe a word of what just went on in that office, I swear to god I *will* break your nose. I will ruin your chances for any college scholarship. Understand?" Micah threatened.

He snarled, "Micah, let's get real here. Don't think for a second that I'm afraid of you and your wimpy little ass."

"You should be. Do we understand one another?"

Jared rolled his eyes. "Yeah, sure," he said and walked away casually.

Micah exhaled deeply and swiveled back to her original direction. The bell rang, signifying the beginning of a new period. Next up, English class.

Chapter Ten

Micah passed a trash can on her way to class and tossed in the ice pack. Her hand was sore and a bit swollen, but the pain had subsided. She took her seat in English. She wasn't surprised by all the whispers and did her best to ignore them. She looked over at Casey, who smiled at her. Micah smiled back half-heartedly and opened her book to the appropriate chapter. Samantha Stevenson strolled in and sat between Micah and Casey.

"Ms. Stevenson, you're late," the teacher said.

She responded with a careless, "Sorry."

"Once more and you stay after school," he chastised her.

"Yes, sir," Samantha said.

Micah couldn't stop herself from stealing glances at Sam. Sam wasn't a bad looking girl but Emily was way prettier. Was Sam late to class because she had been with Emily?

Without warning, Sam turned to face Micah and handed her a note. Micah peered over at Casey, assuming she sent it, but Casey was watching the teacher. Micah took the note and read it. "Emily told me you know. Thanks for not saying anything. – S."

Micah looked up to find Sam staring at her. "Sure thing," Micah said meekly.

The girl Emily had been sleeping with for nearly an entire year was sitting right next to her this whole time. And Micah had been completely clueless. She couldn't process it. Micah didn't hear a word the teacher said during the whole class.

The bell rang for lunchtime. As everyone was leaving, Micah approached Casey to head down to the locker room together.

Casey shot her a charming smile. "I have to hit up my locker first. Meet you down there?" Casey asked.

Micah smiled too. "Okay."

Micah was waiting in a dry shower stall when Casey appeared and closed the curtain. Before Micah could ask what this meeting was about, Casey engaged Micah in a very long kiss. Casey pulled back and grinned.

"I've been waiting since Saturday to do that," Casey confessed while taking Micah's swollen hand between her own two hands. "How's it feeling?"

Micah was still trying to catch her breath. "Casey, there's so much going on. I don't know what to do or who to talk to and I can't..." Micah choked up and swallowed hard. Casey kissed Micah's hand and then let it go.

"Micah, you can tell me anything."

"I came out to my mom over the weekend."

Casey let out a laugh of excitement, wrapped her arms around Micah, and then kissed her again. "That's awesome! Good for you! How did it go?"

Micah shrugged. "Well"—she paused—"she knows we slept together."

Casey frowned. "You really do tell your mom way too much."

Micah let out a laugh. "Not like that. She assumed and I didn't call her bluff."

"She must hate me!"

"Oh, no." Micah put her hand on Casey's shoulder. "She doesn't hate you. I promise."

Casey nodded. "That took valor. I'm proud of you."

"Thanks, but there's more," Micah said.

"What?"

Micah stared at the showerhead above them. It was old and rusty. Then she focused her gaze on Casey. "After I hit Jared, Mr. Lewis called my mom. She outed me."

Casey's eyes went wide. "Mr. Lewis knows?"

"Yeah, seems that way."

"Why would your mom do that?"

"I'm not quite sure."

"Wait, why didn't you just tell him that Jared said something about Emily?" Casey inquired.

"It's complicated," Micah said.

Casey crossed her arms. "I have fourteen more minutes. Go."

Micah groaned. "Emily's family life is rough. If she got in trouble they'd call her parents, and nothing good would come from that. I tried to keep her name out of it."

"Oh, so you put yourself in a position to be outed for your best friend. Yet you steered clear of me so that no one would think you're gay? What the hell is that?" Casey started to leave, but Micah captured her arm and pulled her back toward the stall.

Casey stopped and turned around. "What?" she asked coldly.

"Casey, it's not like that." Micah rested her hand on Casey's waist. "It's not you against Emily. That's just the way it happened. I'm sorry."

Casey's expression lightened. "Micah, I wanted to meet you here for a reason."

Micah waited and Casey continued, "Remember when we were talking on the phone, and we agreed that things didn't happen for us the way we both wanted?"

"Yes, I remember."

Casey's lips tightened and a sigh escaped. "Will you go out with me?"

"What?"

"I'm sorry. I'm bad at this. I've never asked anyone out before. So, will you?" Casey repeated.

Micah stared silently into Casey's dark, beautiful eyes. She couldn't resist the idea of having a girlfriend.

Casey went on, "I was going to ask you out Friday night while we were at your house, but things got all chaotic. And then you came over, and…well, it just happened and I lost my nerve." Casey took a deep breath. "I don't want you thinking that your first time was with someone you weren't officially dating. That seems like something that would bother you."

Micah stuttered, "I know it's totally geeky, but I—"

Casey pressed her index finger over Micah's lips. "Micah, in my heart, we *were* dating when we slept together. So I'm asking you now to make it official." Casey's cheeks flamed. "See? I can be a geek too."

Micah smiled and took Casey's finger off her lips. She leaned over and kissed Casey on the corner of her mouth. "Yes, I will go out with you. Thank you for asking."

Casey glowed. "Excellent!"

The bell rang, ending lunch period and beckoning them to class. They hugged and Casey whispered in Micah's ear, "Best day ever. I'll talk to you later, okay?" She kissed Micah on the cheek.

"Okay," was all Micah could get out.

Casey, about to leave, pointed to Micah's swollen hand. "Good thing you're a lefty," she said and winked, then vanished.

Casey's words dumbfounded Micah. Still in shock, she picked up her bag and headed to class.

Micah opened up her history book as Emily took the seat next to her. Micah looked up and their eyes met.

Emily rubbed her thumb over her own top lip, motioning for Micah to do the same. "You have got to learn to check yourself in the mirror," she teased, as if nothing had changed between them.

Micah quickly rubbed her mouth with her sleeve.

"It's gone," Emily assured her. "How's the hand?"

Micah rotated it. She could move her fingers again, though that caused some pain. "It's healing. How's the eye?"

Emily touched her bruise. "Looks worse than it feels."

The teacher walked in and began unpacking his briefcase.

"Did you read my note? Will you meet me at the library?" Emily asked.

Micah's shoulders drooped. "Okay, but I literally only have one minute. I can't miss my bus or my mom will have a fit."

Emily offered a meager smile as the teacher started to speak. She faced the front of the classroom and

Micah studied her profile. Micah was still grappling with the image of Emily and Sam kissing.

Her mind flashed to the last time Emily had slept over Micah's house. Emily had convinced her it would be a good idea to make a batch of brownies. Being the amateur chefs that they were, they had gorged on the batter until there was nothing left to bake. A food fight involving several spatulas and a lot of chasing had left chunks of brown goo in Micah's hair. Emily had spent hours helping her wash it out painstakingly, one tress at a time. They had fallen asleep in the bathroom after a long bout of unyielding laughter. That night, Emily had confided in Micah about losing her virginity. Micah began to reconsider her mother's advice on forgiveness.

Micah passed the rest of her classes in a similar haze. She barely paid attention to any of her teachers. If quizzed, her grade point average would be tarnished. The school bell rang and the day finally ended.

Micah picked up her backpack, multiple notebooks, and her deteriorating copy of *Othello*, and then she headed for her locker. Casey was waiting for her in the same spot Emily traditionally stood. As Micah arrived, she saw a smile form on Casey's face, and couldn't help but smile back.

Micah opened her locker and whispered to Casey, "What are you doing here?"

Casey slid a piece of paper into Micah's pocket, causing a spike in Micah's heart rate. Micah's mouth opened slightly, but Casey just winked and trotted away. Emily suddenly rounded the corner. Micah, aghast, watched as the two of them crossed paths and blatantly looked at one another with curiosity.

Emily nodded hello as she came closer to where Micah stood.

"Hey. I thought we were going to meet in our spot," Micah said.

"I figured we could head there together. You know, to give us more time to talk."

Micah shut her locker. "Sounds good."

The two of them walked down the hallway. When they were freshmen, they had discovered an isolated niche of the library. It was dank; but shelves of dusty eighteenth century literature shielded them from the masses, creating a quintessential place to meet and swap scandalous stories about their peers. Without any need to guide each other, they entered their reserved hideout. Once there, they stood face to face.

"I have so much to say to you," Micah started.

"I figured as much."

"Emily, when I came out to you, you said things...you said things that made it seem like it was just me who was different. You even acted surprised when you already *knew*! Why the hell did you do that to me?" Micah whispered harshly.

"Micah, I'm sorry that this all went down the way it did. But you have to believe me! I would never hurt you. And I *was* surprised when you came out to me. In a good way. I had been waiting a long time for you to figure it out. Like I said before, I really wanted you to discover for yourself who you were, because—"

"Because why, Emily? You can never get to the part where you tell me why."

Emily took Micah's hand, catching her off guard. Emily's touch made Micah jump, but she didn't pull back. Their eyes locked.

"Because I've liked you ever since I knew that I was gay. And if by some chance you felt the same, I wanted you to come to me on your own. I didn't tell you, because I was scared that you would be totally freaked by the idea that I had a crush on you." Emily was shaking.

Micah's mouth went dry. "Emily."

"Micah, I'm sorry I didn't tell you. I couldn't risk losing you. But I guess it doesn't matter, because I lost you anyway."

Micah shook her head robotically. "I don't understand."

"It's a lot. I know," Emily sympathized.

"But Friday you said the reason you hook up with Sam is because your heart belonged to…"

"You," Emily said.

"Em, your heart? That's not something you say about a crush."

Emily smiled sadly. "I know."

Micah imploded internally.

"Okay, uh, well, then why did you work so hard to get me to go out with Casey?"

"Because, Micah. When you care about someone, you try not to be selfish. You realized that you had feelings for Casey and not"—Emily looked away, took a breath, and then looked back—"As your friend, I had to respect that. I want you to be happy. No matter what it takes."

Emily's speech smothered Micah with an agonizing warmth. Micah realized Emily still had her hand and she slowly released herself from Emily's grip. Emily tried to stay poised.

"You slept with her, didn't you?" Emily asked. "When you didn't come home Friday night?"

Micah checked over her tattered sneakers. She took a deep breath. *How would Emily know that?* She looked up at Emily. "How did you...?"

Emily pointed to Micah's ear. "I see you've got your earring back."

Micah had two instantaneous flashbacks: Emily at her house noticing it was missing to begin with and Emily in the principal's office when Casey returned the earring to Micah.

"She's my girlfriend now," Micah informed.

Emily pressed her lips together and forced a smile. "I'm happy for you."

"Thanks." Micah wilted. "Emily, you encouraged me to pursue this, you know."

Emily let out a hurtful laugh. "Yeah, I suppose I did."

"Emily?"

"Yes?" Emily tilted her head.

"I'm sorry for being a jerk. I do forgive you. You're still my best friend," Micah said faintly.

Emily wrapped her arms around Micah tenderly, then pulled away. Emily's cheek lingered on Micah's, but only for a second. A strange sensation coursed through Micah before Emily stepped back completely.

"Thank you. I appreciate that. I need some space, though," Emily stated.

Micah winced. "What? Why?"

"I didn't realize how badly it would hurt to see you with Casey." Emily started to walk away.

"Emily, wait!" Micah said in a panicked hush. "You can't leave me." Micah showcased her battered hand. "I hit someone for you."

Emily smiled and lowered Micah's arm down for her. "That was sweet of you. I would bust someone up for you, too. But I need time." Emily took more steps toward the door.

"Emily!" Micah called out in a loud whisper, causing a few students to look up briefly.

Emily stopped and turned around. "What?"

"I came out to my mom." Micah tried to smile.

"That's great, Micah. I'm proud of you."

Micah watched Emily's silhouette drop out of sight. Evidently, "I'm proud of you," was the standard response to coming out. She had no time to think about it further. She had a bus to catch. Micah swung her bag over her shoulder. She raced to the front of the building, where she watched the bus pass by.

She looked up at the sky. "What the hell?" She grabbed her phone to call her mom, but its battery had died. A despondent Micah started for home on foot.

Chapter Eleven

Micah walked through her front door about forty-five minutes after leaving the school. Mrs. Williams was sitting on the couch, drumming her fingers against the coffee table. Before Micah could explain or apologize, her mother pointed to the clock.

"You were supposed to come home right after school! That was our agreement, Micah." Her mom stood up. "Where exactly *is* my daughter? First you're lying about where you are, then you're telling me about a very big discovery about yourself. And today, you're punching people at school and can't even manage to make it home on time?" Now her mother was shouting.

"Mom, I didn't mean to. I missed the bus and my cell phone's dead." Micah handed her mom the phone as proof. "I just walked home."

"Micah, I've never worried about your ability to make choices. I have never mistrusted you, but I'm really starting to have my doubts. You're not yourself."

"I'm sorry. Can we sit down, please? I'm exhausted," Micah pleaded. The two of them headed to the couch and sat facing one another.

"What happened at school today, Micah?"

Micah cleared her throat. "Mom, I told you. I hit Jared because he's a jerk. It was the wrong thing to do."

"Micah, that sort of behavior is inexcusable."

"I know, Mom. I said I was sorry. But why'd you tell the principal I was gay?"

Micah's mom shook her head. "I don't know. I guess I thought it was the best way to keep you looking as innocent as possible. You were worried about what could happen at school, as you should be. Kids are mean. This world, although it's much better than years before, is still not a safe place for people who deviate from the norm. God forbid you were attacked at school or something. I want you to be yourself, but I want to know that you'll always be safe. No one can guarantee me that, which is the hardest part of being a parent."

"I didn't mean to scare you."

Micah would deal with the consequences of being outed when that time came. It wasn't worth fighting over. She embraced her mom and they shared a long hug.

They pulled apart. "Am I grounded even more now?" Micah asked, folding her hands on her lap as if in prayer.

"No. But no more slip-ups. We have to try to get through this together as a family."

"Okay."

Her mother nodded. "Go charge your phone and do your homework."

Micah went upstairs to her room and closed the door. She reached in her pocket and took out the note that Casey had placed there. It was one line of words strung together, "You have the softest lips." Beneath the sentence was an outline of Casey's lips, the same color as her lip gloss. Apparently this was becoming Casey's signature. Micah touched her own lips, but didn't feel that they were anything special. She put the note back in her pocket.

Micah took a breath and tried to calm herself down. She slowly rose to her feet and glanced over at the picture of her and Emily on her desk. She picked it up and touched it with her hand. She studied Emily's eyes and her smile. *I can't believe she needs space from me.* She put the picture down before she started getting overly emotional again.

Get a grip. You've got this, she told herself. *You have a girlfriend who is into you and everything is fine.* She looked up at the image of Blonde Crusader on her wall. "I'll be fine, right?" she asked the poster.

Micah picked the picture back up and shoved it into a drawer. She sat on her bed, rummaged through her bag, and dug out all of the homework she had to finish for tomorrow. It was going to be a long week.

Micah committed to exceeding her parents' expectations for the rest of the week. She had done all of her homework, studied extra hard to preserve her spot on the honor roll, and was home on time after school got out. She made it a point to take out the garbage, do the dishes each night, and even matched the plastic storage lids to their containers.

She embraced her isolation. Aside from a few notes passed here and there and one makeout session in the girls' locker room on Wednesday, she hadn't had much contact with Casey. Emily avoided her altogether.

On Thursday morning, Micah was finishing her breakfast in the kitchen alone, when her mom sat across from her. Micah checked the time to make sure she didn't miss the bus.

"Micah," Mrs. Williams started, "I can't believe I'm doing this."

"What, Mom?"

Her father entered the kitchen, smiled at Micah, and went to pour himself a cup of coffee. Micah's mother continued speaking. "Your father and I recognize how hard you've been trying this week, and we realize that you've been going through a lot. We decided that your punishment is over."

Micah's mouth dropped open and she glanced up at her father, who just winked at her. Micah looked back at her mom. "Seriously?" She beamed giddily.

Her mother nodded. "Seriously. But you have to keep working just as hard. Okay?"

"Yes!" Micah jumped up and threw her arms around her mother.

Then Micah ran over to her dad, who put his coffee down and squeezed her. "Be good. Don't make me look bad," he whispered in her ear. Micah kissed him on the cheek.

"Definitely," she agreed. She grabbed her cereal bowl and put it in the sink.

"I've gotta catch the bus. I love you both. You guys are the greatest!" she whooped as she ran out the door. She jogged to the bus stop, full of energy. Remarkably, the bus arrived on time and the ride was quick.

Chapter Twelve

As Micah approached the school entrance, she spotted Emily lying on the grass outside, listening to her MP3 player. Her tutoring session must have ended early. Micah walked closer to where Emily lay. She kept what she thought was a safe distance. Emily's eyes were closed and her full lips glistened in the sunlight. Her shirt had ridden up a little and Micah could see her navel ring. Micah crept closer, but then saw Sam coming towards Emily from the opposite direction. Micah quickly made her way behind a tree and watched.

Sam sat next to Emily and pulled one of the earbuds out of Emily's ear. Micah knew how much Emily hated that and waited for an angry reaction. When Emily opened her eyes and smiled, Micah pouted. She watched Emily sit up, and then honed in on how close Sam's hand was to being on top of Emily's. Their heads were bent together and they were giggling. Before Micah could even attempt to decode their conversation, she heard her name called out.

"Hey, Micah!" Casey shouted, sprinting over to her. Micah cringed as both Emily and Sam glanced over to where Micah was standing. Emily narrowed her brows at Micah and then refocused on Sam. Casey greeted Micah by placing her hand on Micah's hip, but just for a second. Micah appreciated Casey's stealthy affection.

"Hey," Micah said. She wanted to kiss Casey, but the fear of being seen held her back. Students had not started talking about Micah's sexuality yet, and she was trying to keep it that way. There was only a rumor that she had multiple personalities, one of which had caused her to unleash on Jared.

"Whatcha doing hiding behind trees?" Casey asked. She followed Micah's gaze and caught sight of Emily and Sam sitting closely.

"Nothing," Micah said casually.

"Oh, I see. They seem pretty cozy," Casey noted.

"I know, right?" Micah agreed, relieved that she was not the only one seeing this.

Casey laughed. "Well, you're her best friend. Don't you know if there's anything going on?"

"No!" Micah barked. "Emily's straight as far as I know."

Casey looked over at Emily and Sam again, and then back at Micah. "Are you sure about that?"

"Of course." Micah pulled Casey a little closer. "Why? Did you hear something?"

Casey laughed. "Relax. I just know that my gaydar totally goes off around Sam, and Sam seems to be digging on your friend there. Soooo, whether Emily realizes it or not, she's being hit on by a chick right now."

Micah peered over at Emily and Sam. "Really?"

"Really."

"Emily and I aren't talking," Micah disclosed.

Casey grazed Micah's arm. "I was going to ask you about that."

"Why?"

"Because you two are *always* together, and I haven't seen her within a hundred feet of you for days now. Is everything okay? Is she cool with us going out?" Casey asked.

"I don't know," Micah said.

"I don't think she is," Casey said with conviction.

"Why do you think that?" Micah leaned against the tree and dug her finger into some sap.

"Your friend decided to pay me a visit before I hit the track this morning," Casey answered breezily.

"What? What did she say?" Micah's hands became clammy.

"She cares about you. That's for sure."

"Casey, what did she say?"

"She told me that I better not hurt you and then she walked away. Very mysterious and gangsta-like," Casey quipped.

Micah covered her face with her hands. "I am so sorry. I can talk to her."

"It's okay. You guys aren't talking and she's probably just bugging out." Casey glanced towards Emily again. "Besides, she might be a little preoccupied."

"How can you be so mature about this situation?" Micah dropped her hands.

"Micah, there's no situation. Anyways, I raised myself and basically raised my dad. I look like a teenager, but in here"—Casey put her hand over her heart—"I'm like seventy."

"I don't get it. It's like I come out and everyone has a gay side," Micah marveled. She backpedaled to protect Emily. "I mean, uh, I know that's not the case, but it just feels that way."

Casey tapped Micah's shoulder. "Come on. We can't be late." Casey led her to the school entrance. "Sometimes when you realize who you are, you realize that you aren't so different."

"You lost me."

"Okay, so it's like this. Let's say you're introduced to, um, a new singer for the first time. You're all, 'Am I the only one who knows how talented he is?' But now that you're aware of him, you go to school and start noticing that other people are listening to his music. Or they're wearing a tee shirt with his name on it, stuff like that. Because you're now tuned in to what's inside of you, it's easier for you to recognize what's *outside* of you. You start seeing other people who are like you, even though you didn't before. Does that help?"

Micah understood. She smiled, finding Casey to be even more attractive by how insightful she was. "Got it."

"Nice. So I'll see you in English?"

"Wait! I have good news," Micah said.

Casey smiled. "Oh yeah? What's that?"

"I'm off punishment."

Casey's smile went from innocent to mischievous. "Oh? So this means you can get out of the house this weekend?"

"Uh huh."

"Great! I'll plan something. You won't be disappointed."

"Casey, what about Emily?" Micah asked.

Casey shrugged. "What about her? I have no intention of hurting you, so I'm not worried. If she really is your best friend, she'll get over the fact that you're with me."

Micah nodded. "Right. Okay."

With that, Casey headed to her homeroom.

As Micah approached her locker, she saw Emily in the hallway talking to Jared. Jared was bent over, his mouth blowing words into Emily's ear. Emily's eyes were attentive. He laughed and she touched his forearm coquettishly. Micah's gag reflex suddenly weakened. Were they *flirting*? She made her way over to them.

"Hi?" Micah said neutrally.

Jared put his arm around Emily, who looked up at him and avoided all eye contact with Micah. "Micah, hey. How's it going?"

The color drained from Micah's face. Before she could speak, Jared gave Emily a quick kiss on the forehead.

"I'll see you later, Em," he said and walked away.

Micah stared at Emily. "'Em'? He calls you 'Em'?" A pang of jealousy stabbed Micah.

Emily held up her hand. "Micah, don't."

"What the hell is going on?" Micah asked with revulsion.

Emily came closer to Micah. "Please don't look at me like that."

"Like what?"

"Jared and I decided to give dating a shot," Emily explained.

"What?" The hallways spun around Micah. "Why?"

Emily shook her head. "It's fine, Micah. Let it go."

"No! Tell me what the hell you're doing with him!" Micah grabbed Emily's wrist. Several students stopped to watch this interaction to see if it would escalate.

Emily pulled her arm away. "It's none of your goddamned business!"

"Well, my life isn't any of your business either! Stay the hell away from my girlfriend with your stupid, empty threats," Micah countered.

"Micah, I'm looking out for you," Emily defended herself, hurt in her eyes.

"Well, I don't need you to." Micah left for homeroom, making it there just as the late bell was sounding.

After attendance was taken and the bell rang, Micah approached Jared. "Can I talk to you for a second?"

"Hey, I didn't touch her against her will," Jared said.

"We had a deal."

"Look, I talked to Emily after your cute little warning on Monday, and *she and I* struck a deal."

"What kind of deal?" Micah could hear her voice shrinking.

"Well, Senior Gala's coming up. I told her that if she acted like she was dating me and went to the dance with me, that I wouldn't tell everyone she was licking Stevenson's pussy or that Stevenson was licking hers," he sneered callously. "Besides, maybe after the dance, she'll give me a little extra something aside from a goodnight kiss."

Micah raised her right fist at him, indifferent to the fact that it hadn't fully healed yet. He just laughed.

"Now, now, Micah, I didn't hurt her. Just like you asked, so you have to play nice," he said.

"She agreed to this?" All the air in the building had gone stale.

Jared leaned in closer. "Listen, I can't have the school thinking I was crushing on some lez. No girl has ever turned me down. I mean, look at me." He pointed to his face as he spoke. "Besides, she's fucking hot."

Micah fought the urge to spit on him.

"Don't your friends already know what's going on? Weren't they in town with you that night? Didn't they ask you why you didn't get in trouble for hitting her?" Micah was outraged.

"Yeah, they were. My friends are dumb. They believe what I tell them to believe. It's simple. I told them that Emily plays for both teams. That she called me the next day to make up, and that she'd choose me over some homo any day." He looked around as the hallways were emptying and then back at Micah. "Sorry, kiddo. You lose."

Micah's eyes seared into the back of him as he sauntered away.

Chapter Thirteen

Micah walked into English class in a daze. She took her seat and was immediately given a note from Sam, which Micah reluctantly accepted.

"Locker room at lunch?" was scribbled in Casey's writing. Micah looked over, forced a smile, and nodded. Sam mouthed the words, "So obvious," with a sly smile, and then turned to face the teacher. Micah was beginning to think that Sam had a very limited vocabulary. She shot Sam a dirty look that went unnoticed.

Micah, waiting for lunch, watched the clocks tick by in all of her classes. None of them were in sync. As her math teacher finished solving an equation on the board, the bell rang. Micah quickly wrote down the homework assignment and made her way to the locker room to meet Casey.

She headed to their designated shower stall. Micah opened the curtain, surprised to find Casey leaning against the back of the stall. Micah studied her. Her deep brown eyes seemed almost black, and her lips were shiny with the lip gloss that Micah never remembered to wipe off. Her long, brown curls hung loosely over her shoulders. Micah slid the curtain shut.

"Hey, stranger," Casey whispered. She grabbed Micah by the hips, pulling their bodies together. Casey's lips pressed hard against Micah's. As they kissed, Casey's hand reached up under Micah's shirt. Micah wriggled away.

Casey opened her arms. "Sorry?"

Micah twiddled with the seam of her cotton jersey. "It's okay. I just…we're in school."

"Yes, I realize that," Casey said. "Look, Micah. I told you I would start over and take it slow, so that's what I'm trying to do. But we keep coming in here, and when we kiss I just…"

Micah waited for her to finish.

"I want to attack you!" Casey's head tilted back. "You drive me insane!" She looked at Micah and smiled. "I'm trying. I'm sorry. It's harder than I thought."

Micah stood silently and listened to the water drip in the stall next to them.

"Can you sleep over tomorrow night?" Casey asked quietly.

"Uh, I'll ask?" Micah wrung her hands. "I can't promise anything."

Casey smiled. "Okay. But until then—" Casey took Micah's hand and put it up to her own cheek, inches away from her glossy lips. Casey closed her eyes and slowly moved Micah's thumb into her mouth, circling her tongue around it. Micah's heart palpitated, gaze transfixed on Casey. The bell interrupted. Casey opened her eyes, kissed Micah's finger, and flashed Micah another smile.

"Something for you to think about. Let me know about tomorrow!" Casey gave Micah a peck on the lips as she left.

The locker room door closed with a bang. Micah stepped out of the shower stall and over to the mirrors. She wiped away the evidence, Casey's lip gloss imprint, from her mouth. Lower jaw protruding, blue eyes enlarged, she tousled her brunette hair. She puckered her lips and tried to emulate Casey's sultry presentation. The result was more of a parody. Micah was not familiar with the stranger staring back at her. Disparaged, she voicelessly chanted a slew of self-deprecating words. She schlepped to class.

The rest of the day went by quickly, and soon Micah was in her last class: history.

As she walked to her seat, she glanced over at Emily. Emily's bruises were almost healed completely. Before Micah could look away, Emily caught her staring.

"What?" Emily asked.

"What?" Micah responded guiltily.

Emily arched her eyebrows. "You're the one who's been staring at me all day. You tell me what."

"What are you talking about? A little conceited, aren't we?" Micah shot back.

"Let's see." Emily counted on her hand. "Outside of school this morning, in the halls, at my locker after lunch, just now." She held up four fingers.

Micah pressed her forehead against her palm and squinted.

Emily smirked. "Look, I tell you this all of the time. You're not good at being discreet."

"Uhh. Oh. Uh," Micah sputtered.

The teacher began talking about a project, distracting the girls' attention.

"I'm going to put you in groups of two. This paper needs to be at least twenty pages long, and it will count as twenty-five percent of your final grade."

The class groaned in unison.

The teacher circuited the room, pairing up students. Contingent on who they were assigned to work with, some students joyfully applauded while others booed and heckled.

The teacher pointed to Micah. "Ms. Williams, you'll be working with Ms. Mathis."

Micah and Emily traded looks of unease. A few weeks ago, this would have been ideal. Now it seemed like a punishment. Emily shook her head as Micah received the instructions from the teacher.

"This is due on Friday, the nineteenth," the teacher said. "Good luck."

The class protested with more griping, because the paper was due on the same day as their dance. The teacher held up his hands in indifference.

After class, Micah caught up with Emily in the hall.

"Emily, can we talk for a second?" Micah asked.

The noticeable hazel rim around Emily's light brown eyes implied that Emily had been crying. Emily looked at her expectantly. "Talk."

"I have to keep my grades up, so we need to work together," Micah explained.

"Oh, so now you need me?" Emily said in a tone Micah had never heard before and hoped never to hear again.

"Uh, yeah. Okay, look," Micah started, "I'm sorry about what I said earlier. I was being—"

"An asshole?" Emily finished Micah's sentence for her.

"Right. That's what I was being and I apologize," Micah said.

"We can ask the teacher for new partners," Emily suggested.

"I think we work well together! Remember last year when we nailed that biology project?" Micah asked excitedly.

Emily gave Micah one of her 'are you serious?' looks and then pulled some books from her locker. "Fine. We can be partners."

"Okay. Do you want to come over Saturday and get started?"

"This Saturday?" Emily asked, annoyed.

"Yes, why? Do you have other plans?"

"I have a date or something."

Micah folded her arms. "With Jared?"

"Yes." Emily zipped her bag and hung it around her shoulder. "But that's at night, so I guess I can come over during the day."

"Okay, how about eleven?"

"Fine," Emily said, walking away. Micah watched as Jared materialized and put his arm around Emily. He shepherded her down the hallway and out of the building.

Chapter Fourteen

As Micah stood there in the corridor, someone grabbed her from behind. She jumped and swerved around to see Casey smiling at her.

"Hey," Micah said.

"What's wrong?" Casey asked.

"Nothing. I was assigned to work on a project with Emily. It's stressing me out since she, like, hates me."

Casey's expression grew pensive. "Maybe this will give you a chance to talk to her?"

"Yeah, maybe. Stranger things have happened."

Casey remained serious. "Listen, Micah, I heard a rumor about Emily."

Micah stagnated. She prayed that no one had revealed Emily's sexuality. "What's that?"

"She's *dating* Jared. Do you know if that's true, because if it's true it's totally fucked up. Why the hell would you date someone who hit you?" Casey's pitch went higher.

"I think it's true," Micah said sadly. "But I'm not even going to bother trying to understand," Micah lied, intending to figure out exactly what was going on.

"Well, that's unfortunate," Casey said.

Micah frowned. "To say the least."

"I have an idea to make you feel better."

"What's that?"

Casey asked, "Do you maybe want to come over my house, seeing that you're no longer grounded?"

"I don't know if asking my parents for too much too soon is a good idea." Micah shook her head.

"Well, just ask. Pleeeease?"

Micah sighed. "Okay, I'll call my mom."

She took out her phone and dialed home. After a few rings, her mom answered.

"Hello?"

"Hey, Ma! How are you?"

"Fine. What do you need?" Her mom didn't hesitate.

"Mom, now that I'm not grounded, may I be authorized to go over Casey's to do some homework?" Micah held her breath waiting for her mom's response.

Casey raised her crossed fingers and Micah smiled.

"Homework or *homework*?" her mom asked, not nearly as naïve as Micah.

"Homework," Micah said flatly.

"Be home by seven for dinner," her mother replied.

A tremor of surprise surged through Micah. "Um, okay. Thanks, Mom." She hung up the phone and saw Casey doing a little victory dance.

"You're kind of weird," Micah pointed out, smiling.

"Ah, look who's talking," Casey said.

Micah got everything she needed from her locker and the two girls headed outside. The sun from earlier was now engulfed by a dense fog. It started to drizzle. There was a bolt of lightning and the benign raindrops rapidly transformed into a downpour.

Micah held out her hand. "Great, it's raining."

"It's water. No big. I have my umbrella," Casey said.

"Do you carry that thing everywhere?" Micah asked.

"Actually I do, because you never know."

Micah smiled. "Sure."

Casey opened her umbrella and held it over the two of them. "Henceforth and onward then!"

Micah rolled her eyes. "Oh jeez."

They headed towards Casey's house. The walk was short, but still gave them extra time to talk.

"So why did you transfer schools?" Micah asked.

Casey shrugged. "My dad decided he didn't feel like paying rent on our last place, so we got kicked out.

The only available apartments were in this area. Not too far from where I was, but far enough to be out of my old school's district. Too bad, because it was an all-girls' school," Casey said and winked at Micah.

"Oh. I see. Were there a lot of gay girls there?"

"A few," Casey said. "Most of the girls were more interested in the boys from the prep school down the street."

"But you weren't?" Micah asked.

Casey stopped walking. "What're you really trying to ask me?"

"Nothing."

Casey moved the umbrella away from Micah and rain began to soak her. Micah yelped as the cold water hit her skin.

"No shelter until you tell me the truth," Casey said, laughing.

"Okay, okay," Micah caved. Casey put the umbrella back over Micah and shook her head.

"You gave in way too easily," she teased.

Micah exhibited a piece of her wet hair. "I *was* having a good hair day, thank you very much."

"Well, you look kind of sexy when you're wet," Casey said. "Now what were you going to ask me?"

"How do you do that?" Micah asked.

"Do what?" Casey began to walk again.

"You say the most overt things without even seeming shy. How?"

Casey smiled. "It's easy. I just say what I'm thinking. Besides, it's extra fun with you, because I always get a reaction."

"What?"

"You are forever blushing. It's really endearing," Casey said.

There was a short silence before Casey started talking again. "So ask me your question."

"Fine." Micah whispered, "Have you ever slept with a guy?"

Casey nodded. "Yes, I have." Micah flinched.

The girls approached Casey's house, made their way to the back door, and then inside. Casey discarded the sodden umbrella on the nearest countertop.

"Is it *better*?" Micah asked.

Casey just looked at Micah. "Better than what?"

Micah shrugged. "Better than sex with girls?"

"It's different. I had a boyfriend for like six months my sophomore year and we slept together a few times. But before him, I already had experience sleeping with girls. I knew once those six months were up that I had to call it off. I wasn't happy. I liked being with girls way better. In *every* way." Casey glanced out the kitchen window then back at Micah. "Does that answer your question?"

"I've never slept with anyone," Micah said, shamefaced as if it were a crime to be a virgin at eighteen.

Casey smiled. "Wrong. You slept with me."

"But never a guy," Micah said.

"Do you want to sleep with a guy?"

Micah shook her head fiercely. "No way."

Casey laughed. "Then who cares? That means you're a gold star."

"A what?"

"A gold star. You identify as a lesbian and you've never slept with a guy. It's a cool thing. Don't freak out about it. Own it," Casey said.

"Huh." Micah gave a small nod.

Casey pointed to the door leading to her bedroom. "Shall we?"

"Should I say hi to your dad?" Micah asked.

"He's not home. He's still at work. Let's get you dried off," Casey said, giving Micah a friendly push.

They headed downstairs and Casey turned on the lights. She fetched a few pieces of clothing and a towel from the closet, and threw them onto her bed. Then she walked over to Micah.

"Hands up," Casey ordered.

"I'm okay," Micah said.

"You're shivering. Put your hands up," Casey said again. Micah mechanically did as she was told and lifted her arms. Casey pulled off Micah's shirt. Micah stood there in her jeans and her bra. Casey took a few steps back and ogled Micah's exposed body. Casey grinned. Micah covered her chest with one hand and went for the towel with the other.

"You know, I could warm you up," Casey offered.

"Thanks, I'll just take the—"

Casey interrupted Micah with a long kiss. "Is this okay?" Casey purred.

"What about going slow?" Micah asked, her voice shaky.

"Oh, right. I keep forgetting that part," Casey whispered, as her hands reached behind Micah to unhook her bra. Micah moved backwards to intercede.

"Casey, I'm serious."

"Okay." Casey grabbed the towel and tossed it to Micah. "Sorry."

Micah wrapped the beige terrycloth around her shoulders. The fibers of her soggy pants glued to her hamstrings. She watched enviously as Casey changed. Fleece pants and a silk shirt were substituted for her moist clothes. Casey nestled onto the bed.

"Get over here, silly," Casey said.

"Uh, I'll just stand," Micah said, looking down at her jeans. Casey laughed and returned to Micah. She took Micah's arms and guided her onto the bed.

"Casey, my jeans, they're—"

"Shh. Do you trust me?" Casey asked as she eased Micah onto her back.

Micah didn't, but she nodded. Casey unbuttoned Micah's jeans, then shimmied them off. Micah lay, awestruck, with only a towel and her underwear covering her.

Casey pointed with a grin to Micah's underwear. "These wet too?" Micah knew what Casey meant and didn't answer.

Casey got on her knees and touched Micah's thighs gently. Micah's body tightened. Casey lowered her head, stopping between Micah's legs.

She looked up at Micah. "Tsk tsk. You have to relax or you won't enjoy it."

"What? No! Wait!" Micah scooched further up on the bed before Casey was able to take off Micah's underwear. "What are you doing?" Micah asked.

Casey looked at Micah with curiosity. "Seriously?"

Micah folded her hands in her lap and looked down at them. "Yeah."

"Whoa. You're really adamant about getting your homework done, huh?" Casey stood up.

She picked up a pair of sweatpants and a hoodie and handed them to Micah. "Here you go."

Micah stood up and put them on, thankful to be covered up and warm again. Once dressed in Casey's clothes, Micah sat down on the bed. She lowered her head. "I'm sorry."

Casey ran her hand along Micah's face. "You don't have to be sorry."

"I feel like an idiot, Casey. I don't think I'm ready for that."

Casey kissed Micah on the cheek. "Well, when you're ready, just say the word." Casey's eyes sparkled.

"Thanks? I'll keep that in mind," Micah said, wishing the bed would swallow her up.

Micah stammered, "I have another question."

"I'm not surprised," Casey joked.

"How will I know when I'm ready for *that*?" Micah asked so softly that she wasn't sure if Casey heard the question.

Casey leaned in closer. "I'm assuming that by 'that' you mean oral sex?"

Micah's cheeks burned and she shrugged.

Casey tipped her head. "I don't know. It's like all the other stuff. You stop thinking with your head and your body kind of takes over. It feels really"—Casey's eyes fell on Micah—"natural. You just know and then it happens."

Micah nodded, biting the nail of her ring finger. "Okay. So what are we going to do for the Senior Gala?" she asked.

Casey sighed. "Getting a little uncomfortable?"

"No, that's not it." Micah crossed her legs. "I just thought of it and maybe now is a good time to discuss it."

"Sure," Casey said doubtfully. "Well, I don't really give a crap what other people think of me, but I respect that you do. We could skip the dance and go on our own date?" Casey gestured to the bed. "Or, we could stay in."

"Are you upset? That I'm not completely ready to be public?"

Casey shook her head. "Nah. I'm just glad that you stopped caring about rumors enough to *date* me. I'm not going to push my luck." Casey paused and blatantly checked out Micah's entire body. "But being a good girl around you is very challenging."

Micah got up from the bed. "I should go." She began taking off Casey's clothes to switch into her own. Casey stood up and stopped Micah from getting completely dressed. She put her arms around Micah's bare waist.

"What if we just do hand stuff?" Casey asked innocently.

"This"—Micah moved her finger back and forth pointing to each of them—"is NOT trying to go slow."

Casey pouted. "Did I hurt you last time?"

"No, it's not that," Micah mumbled. "I'm sorry, Casey. Not right now." Micah pulled away and finished getting dressed.

"Shit, Micah," Casey muttered.

Micah picked up her bag and went up the stairs, calling down, "Bye! I'll ask my mom about tomorrow."

Micah shut the door to Casey's bedroom behind her. The still-wet clothes chilled her body. Her heart thundered. She jogged out of Casey's house, quickening to a sprint when she made it to the sidewalk. The rain drenched her as she fled.

Chapter Fifteen

Micah had been trekking for nearly an hour. Her clothes stuck to her from all the rain, irritating her skin. Her shoes squished and her hair was matted. A few blocks back, she had had to stop herself from going to Emily's house. The roadways were so desolate. She finally reached her front door and slowly opened it, but did not go in. She didn't want to get the floors all wet.

Mr. Williams's gaze flitted up from the laptop on the coffee table. He saw Micah and sprang from the armchair.

"Honey, get in here and close the door! Stand right there." He pointed to the doormat, then ran over to the linen closet. He retrieved a towel and swooped it around Micah. She was trembling. Her mother rushed into the room. She gasped at the sight of Micah and stopped short.

"Oh, Micah! What happened?" her mother asked. She looked at her husband. "Can you give me and Micah a minute?"

Micah's father nodded. "Sure," he said and receded.

"Micah, talk to me."

Drying herself off with the towel, Micah sighed. "I left Casey's early. I thought it would be a good idea to walk home." Micah kicked off her sneakers. "You know, clear my head and stuff," she added casually.

"In a storm?" her mother asked suspiciously.

"Well, I didn't realize how badly it was raining until a few minutes into my walk. I didn't want to burden you and Dad, because you guys have been really great about everything."

"Micah, next time please call. There's no need to walk around in the rain like a hobo. Now you have an hour and a half to shower and get down here for dinner," her mother said. She then took the towel from Micah and dried Micah's hair more thoroughly. "You're okay, though, right?"

Micah nodded. "I'm fine. A warm shower sounds great," she said and went upstairs.

Once Micah got into the bathroom, she peeled off her wet clothes and hustled into the flow of scalding water. She let the warmth run over her. Her thoughts floated to an old movie she watched with Emily a few years ago. There was a scene in it that really skeeved her out. A man was giving his wife an amorous spiel, but coercing her to sleep with him. After a scuffle, the woman gave in. Micah loathed that man. Would it have been different if both characters were of the same sex?

She idled beneath the showerhead until her fingers pruned. She got out and dried her hair, then she lay on her bed. She pulled a blanket around her raw body. Her eyes began to close.

Micah's bedroom door opened.

"Hey you," a familiar voice said.

"How'd you get in here?" Micah whispered. The room was dark.

"Shh." Micah felt warm lips graze against her neck. The lips slowly moved up to meet her own, nearly drowning her in a passionate kiss. Equally warm hands found their way under Micah's shirt, gently turning Micah over onto her back. The hands traced Micah's breasts and found their way to the top of Micah's sweatpants. Suddenly, the lips pressed against hers again, and Micah wanted badly for those lips to consume her. Fingers pulled down her sweatpants, along with her underwear. A tongue slid across her stomach and down to her thighs. Micah's body went limp as the warm hands grabbed her hips.

Micah moaned from deep within her throat, waking herself up. Her eyes shot open and she surveyed the room. No one else was there and she was still curled up in a ball. Micah's heart raced. She had been dreaming.

"Again?" she whispered to herself, unnerved.

She sat up and grabbed her phone. She dialed Casey's number and waited. After four rings, Casey picked up.

"Casey!"

"Micah, hey! I was going to call you, but I wanted to give you some time to cool down. I'm so sorry about earlier," Casey said.

"It's okay. Don't worry about it. I just wasn't there yet," Micah explained, still sleepy.

"I understand. I shouldn't have made you feel pressured," Casey said. "Are you okay? You sound out of breath."

"I…I'm fine. I was calling to make sure things were okay between us. And to tell you that I'm sorry for running away. That seems to be the only thing I'm good at these days."

Casey laughed. "Well, not the *only* thing." After Micah did not respond to Casey's comment, Casey continued, "No worries. I'm glad I didn't scare you away for good."

"No." Micah shook her head. "You didn't."

"Micah, are you sure you're okay?" Casey asked.

"Uh yeah, I'm good. Listen, I'll ask my mom about tomorrow night and I'll let you know."

"Sounds good," Casey said, still unsure about Micah's disposition. "Call me if you need me?"

"Sure. Have a good night."

"You too, cutie," Casey said and hung up.

Micah placed the phone on her pillow, noticing how late it was. She extricated herself from the blanket and stood up. She walked over to her bookshelf and picked up her dream dictionary. She stared at the moons and stars on its cover for a minute.

"Micah!" her mother's voice called.

"Yeah?" Micah yelled back.

"Dinner!"

Micah put the unopened book back on the shelf and headed to the kitchen.

There was a casserole dish and a salad bowl waiting on the table, surrounded by wicker placemats.

Her mother stared over at her. "Did you fall asleep?"

"Yeah, I'm beat." She glanced between her mother and father. "But I wanted to ask you guys something."

"And what might that be?" her father asked.

"Can I sleep over Casey's tomorrow night? Her dad is making dinner," she lied. "I guess it won't be ready until late, so I think I should pack for the night just in case."

Micah watched her parents look at one another doubtfully.

Micah's mom sighed. "Micah..."

"Mom, please. I'm telling you where I'm going to be, when I'll be there, and who I'll be with. And I have to be home fairly early on Saturday before Emily gets here anyways." Micah finished and took a bite of lettuce.

Her mother's eyes lit up. "You and Emily finally made up?" she exclaimed happily.

Micah made a face that did not match her mother's enthusiasm. "Well, not exactly. We were paired up for a history project and neither of us wants to fail."

Mrs. Williams's face fell. "Oh. Well, it's a start," she said and sat at the table.

There was silence. "Mom? Dad?" Micah said. They both looked up at her.

Micah cleared her throat. "Tomorrow night? Can I stay over Casey's?" She waited, then added for good measure, "Please?"

Her mother glanced at her father, who shrugged. "She's not grounded anymore," he pointed out.

Mrs. Williams looked at Micah. "Errr. Fine. Your father and I need to ask something of you, too," she said.

Micah looked up, surprised. "What?"

"Your father and I have been thinking for a while now about maybe purchasing a cottage on the Cape," her mother began.

"Really?" Micah responded excitedly. "This is new?"

"Not really," her father interjected. "We've been saving since you were little and the market is doing well. So we bought," he explained triumphantly.

"So," her mother continued, "for the next few weekends, your father and I will be at the cottage, cleaning it and getting it ready. This way when summer rolls around, it'll be good to go. Can we trust you to be alone for the next few weekends? We'll leave you money for food and the keys to my car."

Micah dropped her fork. "You're serious?" she asked. "Of *course* I can handle the weekends alone!"

"Micah, listen. Your father and I are feeling iffy given your recent behavior, so we are really counting on you to hold down the fort. You CANNOT screw this up or you WILL be grounded again." Her mother's voice was steady and serious.

"Yes, Captain! I accept this mission," Micah said, laughing softly. She noticed that her father chuckled as well. Her mother gave them both looks of disapproval.

"Okay, it's settled. Starting this weekend, you'll be on your own. I'll make sure that Mrs. Foster next door knows, so that, god forbid, you can call her in case of an emergency," her mom said.

"I'll be fine," Micah assured. In her head, she was mimicking Casey's victory dance from earlier.

Chapter Sixteen

Micah woke up Friday morning before her alarm went off. No longer fatigued, she yawned and vivaciously outstretched her arms. The week was coming to a close!

She prepped for the hours ahead, starting with a short shower. She pulled her brown hair up into a messy ponytail, then threw on her jeans and a frayed band tee shirt. Next, Micah ransacked her dresser drawers, analyzing her pajama options for that night. She didn't own anything provocative, which was probably for the better. Something conservative, sweatpants and a tank top, would suffice. She crammed everything into her overnight bag and headed downstairs.

"Good morning!" she said cheerily as she entered the kitchen.

Her mother looked at her with one raised eyebrow. "Good morning. Are you okay?"

"I'm fine. Why do you ask?" Micah responded, pouring herself a glass of milk.

"You generally aren't this perky in the morning," her mother observed.

"I had the best night's sleep!" Micah grabbed a banana off the counter and chugged the entirety of her milk. "And now I'm off to school!"

"You'll be half hour early," her mother informed.

Micah glanced up at the clock. "It's okay. I have a chemistry test today. I can hang in the library and study for it." She kissed her mom on the cheek. "Don't forget. I'll be at Casey's tonight."

"Believe me, I have not forgotten. And you don't forget that your father and I will be leaving shortly after you get home tomorrow morning."

"Got it. Love you!" she called behind her as she left.

Micah bolted to the bus stop and nabbed the early bus. She spent the majority of the commute skimming her chemistry notes. She hated chemistry. Cleverly, she had befriended classmates who excelled at this subject. They willingly helped her when necessary, but she still had to work hard to pass. She was in the midst of highlighting nearly every paragraph on a handout when they pulled up to the school. She assembled her belongings and got off the bus.

The sun had returned and a refreshing breeze clipped her. There were hardly any students convened around the building. Micah was about to take a left towards the library entrance when she noticed Emily lying in the grass again. Micah looked around cautiously for signs of Sam, or Jared, for that matter. *Coast is clear.*

Micah skulked over to where Emily was. She could hear the music coming from the earbuds. Micah hovered above Emily, taking in the details of her features. From this angle, her countenance was faultless. Her cheekbones were set high. Her bottom lip was somewhat thicker than the top one. There was a small freckle on the right side of her neck. Emily's blond hair scattered over the books she was using as pillows.

Emily realized that a shadow had cast over her and she opened her eyes. Perplexed, she squinted up at Micah. She extracted the earbuds.

"Um, good morning? You're here early," Emily said, sitting up. She smirked at Micah's bags. "Do you have a meeting in the locker room?"

Micah gulped. "What? No. I came here early to study." *How did she find out about that?* Micah asked herself.

"Sure. Me too." Emily laughed, pointing to her MP3 player. Micah reached down towards Emily's face. Emily fell silent. Micah pulled a leaf out of Emily's hair and handed it to Emily.

"Here."

Emily took the leaf. "Thanks?"

"You're welcome," Micah said and sat down next to her. Micah went on speaking, "Hair leaves are so last season."

Emily let out a small laugh, then gave the vicinity a once-over.

"What were you listening to?" Micah asked.

"Micah, look, you should go. I'll see you in history, okay?" Emily said.

"Oh." Micah stood up and shrugged. "Right. Sure." She turned around and was facing Sam.

Sam looked Micah up and down. "Nice shirt," she noted.

Micah nodded. "Per our discussion in English."

"Of course," Sam said.

"Well, see you later, Emily," Micah said, walking backwards and waving. She gave Sam a quick nod. "Sam." Sam nodded back as Emily waved.

At that moment, Micah tripped on a rock and stumbled backwards. "Fabulous," she groaned to herself as several passersby giggled.

"Micah! You okay?" Emily called out.

Micah scrambled to get up. Her face scorched. She brushed herself off. When Micah looked up, Emily was standing directly in front of her. Emily was clearly trying to hold back a laugh.

"Are you okay?" Emily asked again.

"I'm fine. Never been better," Micah said, picking her bags off the ground.

Emily reached up and touched the side of Micah's head. Micah closed her eyes.

"Here," Emily said.

Micah opened up her eyes. Emily was handing her some grass. "The grass-y head look went by the wayside along with the hair leaves. Or so I've been told." Emily grinned.

Micah took the green blades from Emily. "Thanks." The girls' eyes met. Micah stared into the brilliant hues of green, light brown, and gold beneath Emily's lashes. They infiltrated Micah's core and something within her quaked.

"Emily, let's go!" Sam called from the distance. Emily held up a finger to Sam, instructing her to wait.

Emily turned back to Micah. "Promise you didn't hurt yourself."

Micah was unable to move. Had that gold always been there?

"Hello? Micah, did you hurt yourself?"

Micah cleared her throat. "Um. No."

Emily started to laugh.

"Hey, don't laugh at me."

"I'm not laughing." Emily doubled over.

Micah started to chuckle and threw the grass that she was holding at Emily. "It's not funny."

"It's totally funny," Emily said as she regained composure. "I have to get going, though. See you later." Micah smiled to herself. Maybe she had her friend back.

Micah finished cleaning herself up in the bathroom. She walked quickly through the halls and made it to her homeroom seat just as attendance was being taken. After the morning announcements sounded throughout the building loudspeakers, Micah headed to chemistry class.

Micah began her test. She worked on the questions one by one. She couldn't even understand what was being asked. She tried to recall the notes she was reading earlier, but kept getting distracted. Instead of picturing equations, her mind fluttered back to her recurring dreams. A student coughed and Micah attempted to refocus. It made no difference. After fifty-five minutes of scientific torture, Micah handed in her exam. There was a slim chance she passed.

Micah stepped out of the classroom to find Casey waiting.

"Hey," Micah said. "Here to walk me to English?" Micah could tell that Casey wanted to kiss her.

Casey smiled. "Why else, my lady?" Casey brushed off Micah's shoulder. "Rolling around in the dirt, are we?"

Micah inspected her clothes. "I sort of fell this morning."

"Ha!" Casey laughed until Micah's frown registered. "I mean, oh. Are you okay?"

Micah smiled. "Yeah. Thanks for your concern."

"Sorry I missed that."

"I'm not. It was so embarrassing and I just washed this shirt," Micah complained as they headed towards English class. "But guess what?" Micah grinned.

"What?" Casey's eyes brightened.

"I can stay over tonight, but I have to be home tomorrow morning by like ten," Micah said.

Casey smiled and squeezed Micah's hand, making sure no one saw the gesture of affection. "I can't wait!" she said as they entered the class and took their seats.

Sitting through the teacher's lecture was painful. Micah successfully avoided Sam for the entire period. Casey didn't pass her any notes so Micah kept her eyes on the clock, counting down the seconds until class was over. The bell rang.

"Finally," Micah mumbled, standing up. She glanced over at Casey, who mouthed an invitation, "Locker room?" For the first time since their locker room rendezvous had started, Micah hesitated.

Once most of the students left the room, Micah approached Casey. "I actually think I'm going to go to lunch today."

"Really? Why?" Casey asked.

"I'm kind of hungry. Besides, aren't your friends wondering where you go every day?"

Casey scoffed at this question. "No. They don't care."

Micah shrugged. "Alright. Well, then aren't you hungry?"

Casey grinned. "Depends. Are you offering me something to eat?"

Micah's cheeks burned and she quickly looked around. The classroom was vacant except for the two of them.

She glared at Casey. "Stop it."

"Okay, okay. I'm sorry," Casey said. "Go get some food and I'll catch up with you later." Casey gave Micah a gentle push towards the door and they went their separate ways.

Chapter Seventeen

Micah pulled her lunch out of her locker and then slammed the door shut. She turned to the direction of the cafeteria and grew nauseated. This feeling was becoming too common for Micah's liking. She placed her hand over her stomach and took a few deep breaths. Was she actually nervous about re-entering the cafeteria? Would Emily be there? Who was Emily even eating lunch with these days? Would people be talking about Micah and Casey?

Micah fended off her anxiety and walked into the lunchroom. She took her seat and emptied her lunch bag. She had not done the best job packing her lunch, as there were only a granola bar and an apple. She sighed and took a bite out of the apple.

She looked around, chewing thoughtfully, as Casey walked by and gave her a wave. Before Micah could wave back, Casey had turned to sit with her friends. They welcomed her with hugs and the chatter among them began immediately. They were all laughing about something. Micah's ears pricked up, but their words remained inaudible. What was Casey telling her friends? Did they know about Micah?

"We both know you can't read lips," Emily said, sitting across from Micah. Emily was looking over at Casey, following Micah's gaze. Micah nearly choked on her apple.

"You good?" Emily asked, watching Micah struggle to swallow.

"I'm good. Thanks," Micah said. "I wasn't sure if you'd be here or not."

Emily shrugged. "Where else would I go during lunch?"

Micah shook her head. "Not sure."

"I don't really find the locker room to be super romantic," Emily said, peeking up from her lunch tray to watch Micah's reaction.

"Well, it is kind of dirty," Micah agreed. The girls smiled at each other. Micah went on, "I didn't mean to bail on you during lunch lately."

Emily nodded. "I get it."

"Soooo, you're talking to me again?" Micah asked, trying not to sound too hopeful.

Emily sighed. "I'm dealing with everything. So yes, I guess this means we're talking again."

Micah exhaled. "Cool."

Emily motioned her head to the contents of Micah's lunch bag. "That's a sad looking lunch," she said, handing half of her sandwich to Micah.

Micah held up her hand to refuse the offer. "It's okay. Thanks, though. I'm actually not really that hungry."

Emily put the food back on her tray. "Suit yourself," she said and continued eating.

"Emily, how come you're not sitting with Sam or Jared?" Micah inquired.

Emily looked up from her food. "Why aren't you sitting with Casey?"

Micah glanced over at Casey and then back at Emily. "I honestly don't know."

Micah felt Emily eyeing her. "What?" Micah asked.

"Nothing." Emily took another bite of her sandwich.

Something in their dialogue resonated with Micah. Countless memories of the same exact exchange suffocated her: Micah catching Emily staring at her. Micah asking, "What?" Emily responding, as she just had, by saying, "Nothing." How did Micah never put the pieces together?

Just then, Jared walked over and took a seat next to Emily. He put a hand up at Micah to greet her and then kissed Emily on the cheek.

"How's my woman?" he said, smiling. Emily rolled her eyes, but then faced Jared and forced a smile back at him.

"Me? Oh, I'm great. And you?" Emily asked dryly.

The sick feeling started to rise again inside of Micah.

"Micah?" Emily's voice seemed far away.

"Huh? What?" Micah uttered.

"You got really pale. Are you feeling okay?" Emily asked.

Micah looked down at her food and immediately realized she couldn't hold onto it. She jumped out of her seat and ran to the bathroom. Several people had stopped to watch, but Micah was oblivious.

Micah got into a bathroom stall and knelt down in front of the toilet. She closed her eyes and retched, tears rolling down her cheeks. Once her body had nothing left to give, she flushed the toilet. She remained on her knees just in case, listening as two familiar voices entered the bathroom.

"Micah?" Casey's voice called out as she knocked on the stall.

"Get out of the way," Emily's voice said harshly.

The door to Micah's stall flew open. Emily crouched behind Micah and began tentatively pulling tendrils of Micah's hair back.

"Are you okay? What happened?" Emily asked.

Micah didn't turn around, but held up her hand. "I'm fine. Please leave."

"Move," Casey ordered Emily. Micah cringed. She listened as Casey stepped forward, and then felt Casey's hand on her back.

"Hey there," Casey said softly to Micah.

Micah nodded. "Hi." She turned around slowly to find both Emily and Casey staring at her. The nausea resurrected.

"Here," Emily said, reaching over Casey to provide Micah with a paper towel. Casey gave Emily a frigid stare.

Casey looked back at Micah. "Are you okay?"

Micah got up woozily. Casey held onto Micah's arm to help balance her.

"Guys, really. I'm okay. It was probably something I ate. I just need a minute," Micah explained.

"You heard her," Casey said to Emily. Emily grimaced.

Micah looked at Casey. "I'm talking to both of you."

"What?" Casey asked.

"Please," Micah begged.

"Let's go," Emily said. She tried to grab hold of Casey, but Casey eluded her grasp.

Casey looked at Micah. "I'll wait for you outside the bathroom."

Micah nodded and watched the girls disappear. She sank onto the cold tile again. She folded her arms across her knees and buried her head there. *This isn't happening*, she tried to assure herself.

After a few minutes had passed, Micah slowly rose to her feet. She walked over to the sink and splashed water on her face. She then tipped her head under the faucet to get a mouthful of water. She rinsed her mouth as thoroughly as possible and spit. She turned the water off as the bell rang to end lunch period.

Micah stepped out of the bathroom and into the lunchroom. Casey stood by the doorway solemnly.

Casey held out Micah's backpack. "Emily gave this to me to give to you. How are you feeling?"

Micah slipped the bag onto her shoulders. "A little mortified and in need of a breath mint. Sorry about all that."

"It's okay," Casey said, reaching into her pocket. She pulled out a piece of gum and handed it to Micah. "Will this do?"

Micah took it and tossed it into her mouth. "Thank you."

"I'm walking you to class," Casey insisted.

"I'd like that. Thanks."

As they left the cafeteria, Micah looked around to see if Emily was anywhere in sight. She wasn't.

Casey noticed Micah scanning the room. "She left with Jared."

"Who?" Micah asked knowingly.

"Emily? She left with Jared. Isn't that who you're looking for?"

Micah shook her head. "No." She fell in step with Casey and pointed to her own mouth. "This gum is great," she said, cracking a smile.

Casey rubbed the top of Micah's head and started to laugh. "Goofball," she said. The two of them continued down the hall.

Micah walked into history class with her head down, fearing the repercussions of the lunchroom incident. The classroom buzz was distinctly void of her name. Only Emily noticed her entrance.

"Feeling better?" Emily asked.

"Working on it," Micah responded, taking her seat.

"Okay then," Emily said, then paused. "Micah?"

"Yeah?"

"What's up with you?" Emily asked. *She just has to know when something's off, doesn't she?*

"It's hard," Micah whispered.

"What's hard?"

Micah sighed. "Seeing you with *him*."

Emily tipped her head sideways. "We'll talk tomorrow, okay?"

"Okay." Micah moved her head up and down in slow motion. *Talk about what?* Micah pondered this for the rest of the day, which dragged. Did time move this slowly in alternate hell dimensions?

Chapter Eighteen

The final bell ended the school week, and a few students in the halls even cheered. Micah beelined to her locker. The weight of her backpack rivaled the weight of her day. Once there, she began to unload. She jammed her chemistry book and a bundle of binders onto the top shelf, building a feeble pyramid. From the toppling mound, she rescued the only book she would need for the weekend: history. Micah strapped the much lighter bag around her shoulders, grabbed her overnight bag, and skipped out of the building. The weekend would be better. She was sure of it.

Micah had agreed to meet Casey outside so that they could walk to Casey's house together. Micah neared Casey, who was laughing.

"Do you have enough luggage for one night?" Casey asked, eyeing the enormous bag that Micah was carrying.

Micah looked at what she was holding. "What? It's only one bag."

Casey kept laughing. "It's gigantic. Let me carry it." Casey held out her hand. Reluctantly, Micah forfeited the bag.

Casey lifted it up and down. "What do you have in here anyway? It's not even heavy."

Micah pointed to the street. "Can we get a move on?"

"Okay, boss," Casey joked and they headed for Casey's house. "I was hoping your mom would okay you staying the night, so I did my best to prepare," Casey said.

Casey stopped and pretended to bench press the bag. "Clearly I didn't prepare as much as you did, but hey, the thought was there."

Micah laughed. "I wanted to be well-equipped in case there was another monsoon. So what did you prepare?"

"You'll see."

The girls began to walk again. A group of kids passed by them on skateboards, whistling. Micah looked at Casey.

"I think that was for you. You've got a relatively extensive fan base. Girls *and* boys," Micah said.

Casey smiled. "I don't know. You're kind of cute yourself in your little band tee shirt from 1985."

Micah was about to defend her taste in music and clothes, but saw that Casey was laughing.

"I'm kidding," Casey assured her.

"I love this shirt," Micah mumbled to the ground.

"And you should. It suits you," Casey said, smiling.

Micah glanced back to where the boys were headed. "Do you think they could tell?"

Casey's brow creased. "Do I think they could tell what?"

"That we're, like, together?" Micah studied Casey, but was unable to read her expression.

"No, I don't think that they could tell. But so what if they could? Does it matter?" Casey's tone was firm.

"It'd be nice if I could…" Micah balked.

Casey stopped walking again to face Micah. "If you could what?"

Micah looked down. "If I could hold your hand and it wouldn't be a big deal."

"It doesn't have to be a big deal." Casey smiled, moved her hand closer to Micah's, and wiggled her fingers. "It's right here for you to hold if that's what you want."

Micah looked at Casey dejectedly. "I can't. I'm sorry."

"You'll get there." Casey smiled. "When the time is right." Casey flicked Micah's hand. "And the person is right." Casey curtsied. "You'll be able to."

Micah smiled back, doubtful. "Perhaps."

"Trust me," Casey said.

They walked another block wordlessly. Casey broke the silence.

"So, you and Emily are speaking again?" she asked.

"Yeah." Micah laughed a little. "I worked my magic and she's slowly coming around."

Casey smiled. "Well, you are one irresistible girl, Micah Williams."

Micah laughed more. "Yes, I'm sure that's it. And the fact that we've known each other since we were five years old has nothing at *all* to do with it."

"That's fair. Do you want to talk about what happened today at lunch?" Casey asked.

"Nope. I'm over it." Casey nodded in acceptance of Micah's response.

Before long, they were approaching Casey's house. Casey reached into her bag, pulled out a set of keys, and unlocked the back door. She motioned for Micah to enter ahead of her, and Micah stepped inside. Casey came in after and closed the door behind them. Casey's dad was snoring in the next room over.

"Sorry about that. He's a loud sleeper," Casey apologized.

"I remember." Micah smiled bashfully.

"Wait right here, okay?" Casey directed, and then went down to her room toting Micah's bags.

Micah stood in the kitchen alone and her eyes roamed around. It was barren. A draft percolated through a small hole in the screen window. Micah heard Casey's dad babbling incoherently in his sleep. Micah envisioned a day in the life of Casey. Did her father ever interact with her? Did she miss her mom? Was she lonely?

Sorrow coursed through Micah. She was grateful when Casey was suddenly standing in front of her, taking her hand.

"Okay. Come with me," Casey said, pulling Micah towards the bedroom.

They made their way down the stairs. Micah lagged on the final step, absorbing the scene before her. Several candles illuminated the small radius of Casey's room in the shape of a heart on the floor. A lilac aroma permeated the air. A soft song played in the background. Casey's candid display of ardor was enchanting.

Micah looked at Casey. Casey was relishing her glorious work. Micah couldn't resist smiling.

"This is sweet," Micah admitted. "You're a master at creating ambiance."

Casey laughed uneasily. "I've never done anything like this for anyone before."

"I'm honored," Micah said.

Casey walked over to the stereo, started the song from the beginning, and then walked over to Micah. "Will you lay down with me?"

Casey positioned herself on the bed. The temptation to deny such a request was too great. *I am such a lesbian*, Micah thought as she moved towards the bed.

"Just feel it," Casey said. She shifted her body so that she was flat on her back staring up at the ceiling and Micah joined her. Micah enclosed her hand around Casey's. The two of them lay still until the song was over. Then, there was just silence. Micah fixated on the shadows the flames created on the walls. Micah wished that Casey would play the song again, anything to fill the quiet air. Casey moved so that she was now on her side, and she stared hard into Micah's eyes. Casey's eyes had never looked so dark before. They were almost a perfect shade of black, Micah's favorite color. Micah was drowning in the irises.

"I need you to know something," Micah said, also turning to her side so that she was able to face Casey.

"Hmmm? What's that?"

"I don't regret what we did the night I came over here. I feel really bad about running away, but it has nothing to do with you or us. It's just that I..." Micah choked up.

"Stop talking. I get it." Casey reached up and tucked Micah's hair behind her ear. She placed her hand gently behind Micah's neck and drew her in for a titillating kiss. Micah pulled away, gasping for air. Her eyes were still closed and her heart pounded.

"I didn't mean to interrupt you." Casey motioned with her hand for Micah to continue speaking. "As you were saying?"

Micah's face flushed and she opened her eyes. "I still don't understand. You're just so…you." Micah held out her hand like she was presenting Casey to an audience. "You could have just about anyone and you choose *me*? I'm so boring," Micah said, her gaze turning down.

Casey placed her index finger on Micah's chest. "Look at me."

Micah looked up. "What?"

"I gravitated to you instantly, because I knew. I knew that you were special. It wasn't a choice. You're very unique, Micah, and that's a turn-on," Casey said. Casey's cheeks turned slightly red.

Micah smiled broadly and her confidence magnified. Her face grew serious. Micah moved her hand towards the button on Casey's jeans. Casey stiffened.

"Micah, what are you doing? I said I'd go slow and I meant it. But you can't tease, because that's just cruel," Casey said, half-smiling, her eyes on Micah's.

"I'm being merciful." Micah's diligent hands freed the button on Casey's jeans and then hastened to unzip them.

Casey grabbed Micah's hand. "Hold up," Casey said.

"What's wrong?" Micah asked, puzzled.

"There's no rush, remember?" Casey said, though her husky voice betrayed her true want.

Micah smiled. "Stop talking," she jested. Micah needed this badly. She climbed on top of Casey and began kissing her again. Casey's breathing grew heavy. Micah slid her hand beneath Casey's underwear. Casey pulled off Micah's shirt and traced her fingernails along Micah's shoulder blades, sending a shiver throughout Micah's body. Micah's eyes were closed tightly as Casey's soft touch became more of a scratch. The kiss intensified. Micah grew more excited by the second. She was familiar with this feeling – it haunted her while she slept.

Casey whispered Micah's name, and Micah opened her eyes, not sure of who or what she had expected to see. When she realized it was Casey, she inhaled sharply.

"Are you okay?" Casey asked breathlessly. Casey placed her hand on Micah's cheek, the bottom half of her body still moving in time with Micah's hand.

Micah smiled as if nothing happened. "I'm fine," Micah assured her. Casey bit her bottom lip and then began to take off Micah's pants.

"Thank god. You feel amazing," Casey said.

Casey's touch set Micah's skin ablaze. Micah reveled in this lust until dawn.

Something soft and warm pressed against Micah's collarbone. She woke, startled.

"It's just me," Casey whispered, her lips inches from Micah's skin. "Good morning."

Micah looked around, her eyes adjusting to the setting. The heart-shaped embers had extinguished. A garment medley littered the bedside. A dim light shone from the top of the staircase. The backdrop was uncannily peaceful.

Micah slowly sat up. She pulled the sheets up to cover herself.

Casey watched, grinning. "Such the modest girl."

Micah smiled sheepishly. "What time is it?"

"It's almost eight," Casey said. "I don't want you to be late getting home. If we head out before my dad leaves for work, I can drive you."

"That would be great. Thanks."

"How are you feeling?" Casey asked.

"Um, good. How are you feeling?"

"I'm great," Casey said.

Micah began to process segments of the night before. "Casey?"

"Mmm?" Casey was tracing the length of Micah's arm with her fingers.

"I'm sorry we didn't—"

Casey sat up and kissed Micah on the cheek. "Believe me, I'm satisfied. There is no need to apologize. I told you that when you were ready you would just feel it. You'll know."

Micah nodded. "Okay."

"Come on. We have about twenty minutes to get you dressed and home," Casey said, getting out of the bed.

Micah watched as Casey put on her track pants and a hooded sweatshirt, and then pulled her hair into a ponytail. Micah didn't move.

"Or you could just stay where you are." Casey laughed.

Micah shook her head, confused. "Sorry."

"Care to share what's on your mind?" Casey asked as she dragged Micah's bags over to her. "I'm not sure which one has your wardrobe in it," she teased.

Micah smiled and unzipped one of the bags, pulling out a pair of jeans and a tee shirt. "Well, Emily is coming over today to work on that project and I feel…"

"Are you nervous?" Casey asked, trying to help Micah find a descriptor.

"No? I think I'm just dreading the project. It's really going to affect my final grade," Micah said.

Casey nodded, eyeing Micah as she dressed. "I can see how that would be stressful." She leaned over and kissed Micah on the lips. "It'll be great when it's done." Casey clasped Micah's hand and pulled her towards the staircase. "Ready?"

Micah nodded. "Ready." The two girls grabbed Micah's belongings and headed for the door.

It was raining hard outside. They quickly threw the bags in the backseat and climbed into the front seat. Casey started the car and pulled out of the driveway. In silence, she took Micah's hand and held it for the entire trip. Micah watched the rain beat against the passenger side window. After a few minutes of driving, they arrived at Micah's house.

"I believe this is your stop," Casey said. She squeezed Micah's hand before letting it go.

Micah leaned in and gave Casey a soft kiss on the cheek. "Thanks. I'll call you later."

"Okay. Later is good. I love you," Casey said. The words slammed the air between them. Casey's face went pale. Micah's stomach dropped. Did Casey love her? Micah was not sure if she loved Casey. Should she say it back?

"I'm sorry. It just kind of slipped out."

"No, it's okay," Micah managed. "I should get inside."

Micah got out and fished her stuff from the backseat. Casey rolled down the passenger side window as the rain poured on Micah.

Casey waved dismissively. "You don't have to call me later."

"I will. Don't worry," Micah advised, already worried herself. The sky rumbled — Micah's cue. "Don't, uh, hydroplane or anything." *What?*

Casey nodded. "Right."

Micah waved good-bye and dashed to her front door, wet bags in tow. She listened as Casey's tires spattered through a puddle. Micah cursed profusely under her breath and went inside.

Chapter Nineteen

Micah's mom looked up from the television and frowned at Micah. "You really need to start bringing an umbrella with you."

"Good morning to you, too, Mom." Micah said, putting her bags on the floor and taking off her muddy sneakers.

"You have good timing at least. Your father and I are leaving early. The weather is causing some traffic on the highway."

"Okay."

Mr. Williams appeared in the living room. He viewed Micah. "Again?"

"I know, Dad. Umbrella."

"Alright," Mrs. Williams commenced. "There's money in an envelope on the counter, along with the car keys. There's plenty of food in the fridge so you should be all set. Come give me and your father a hug. Then go dry off so you don't catch a cold," her mother ordered.

"Yes, ma'am," Micah said, putting her arms around her mom.

Micah went over to Mr. Williams and gave him a peck on the cheek. "Bye, Dad."

"Later, alligator," he responded.

"No, Dad. No." Micah shook her head.

He laughed and patted her on the back. Her parents headed out the front door.

"We'll see you tomorrow. Behave!"

Once Micah was sure that they were gone, she stripped out of her wet clothes in the middle of the living room. She tossed them over to where she had left the rest of her dampened things. She was about to head upstairs to take a shower when the doorbell rang.

"Seriously?" Micah groaned. She pulled the quilt off the sofa, wrapped it around herself like a towel, and made her way over to the door. She peeked through the window to see that it was Emily.

"Hello?" Micah called out.

"Micah! It's Emily. Can I come in?"

Micah opened the door a crack and stood behind it.

"Emily," she whispered, "get in here, but don't open the door all the way."

Emily slid through the small opening Micah created. Micah swatted the door shut as soon as Emily was inside. Emily stood there and stared at Micah's attire.

"Dare I ask?" Emily grinned.

Micah glanced over at the clock and back at Emily. "You're early. By a lot."

"Well, Mom and Dad got a head start on fighting this morning, so I figured I'd come here." Emily put her backpack down and opened it, pulling out a brown bag. She looked up at Micah, smiling.

"I brought bagels. Your favorite."

"Your early arrival has been approved. Only because I'm starving," Micah said, smiling back.

Emily pointed to the quilt. "Do you maybe want to get dressed?"

"Yes." Micah nodded. "Yes, I do." Scarlet suffused Micah's face. "Ah. How about you go in the kitchen and I'm going to take a super quick shower. I'll be back down here in a few minutes. With clothes on. Help yourself to anything," Micah said and scurried up the stairs.

After the shower, Micah stared into her closet, analyzing her uninspired assortment of apparel. *Why does it even matter what I wear?* She dressed in her staples: jeans and a long-sleeved jersey. She sat on her bed, dawdling over the dilapidated hem of her pants. *It's homework. That's it. The Revolutionary War. General George Washington. Some other elderly gents with wigs.*

There was a knock at her door.

"Micah, it's me," Emily said.

"Yup. It's okay. You can come in."

Emily opened the door, holding a plate with bagels and cream cheese on it.

"Here. I toasted them while you were in the shower."

Micah moved from her bed and sat on the floor, signaling for Emily to sit across from her. Emily sat down and put the plate between them.

"Thanks for doing that," Micah said.

"Sure." Emily took a bite of her bagel. "Where are your parents?" she asked once she was done chewing.

"They actually won't be around for a few weekends. They bought a place on Cape Cod and they're fixing it up," Micah explained.

Emily's eyes widened. "Wow! That's pretty cool. So you have the whole house to yourself?"

"Uh huh," Micah said, spreading cream cheese on her bagel.

"Casey must be liking that arrangement."

Micah scowled at Emily. "Em, Casey doesn't know. No one knows except you. I want to keep it that way."

"Why don't you want your girlfriend to know you're home alone?" Emily asked curiously.

"I just don't, okay?" Micah said abrasively.

Emily shrugged. "Sorry."

"No, I'm sorry. That was uncalled for." Micah finished her food. "Thanks for breakfast. Do you want to get started on the project?"

"Well, first there's something I want to talk to you about," Emily said. She reached up and placed her thumb on the corner of Micah's top lip. Micah's heart thumped.

"You have some cream cheese left over." Emily moved her finger away and sat down across from Micah again.

Micah lowered her head and she put her hand over her mouth.

"It's gone," Emily assured her.

"Thanks," Micah said, still staring at the floor.

"So can we talk for a minute?" Emily asked.

Micah looked up. "Oh. Right. Yes, sure. Talk."

Emily's eyes slanted quizzically at Micah. "Okay? I want to tell you why I agreed to go out with Jared."

Micah froze.

Emily went on, "I have to ask you something, though."

"Okay." Micah became queasy.

"The day you punched Jared, did you out yourself?"

Micah looked at the hand she had used to hit Jared, which was no longer discolored or puffy.

"I had to."

"Why?" Emily asked.

"Because I made you a promise," Micah answered. "I promised you that no one would find out about you. When the principal asked me to explain myself, I knew I had to leave you out of it. My mom had already told him I was gay. She was trying to justify my actions for me. So I went along with it. I thought it made sense to let him believe I was defending myself. If he knew you had anything to do with it, then your parents would've gotten involved and that would've been a disaster. I couldn't let that happen."

"So you put your reputation on the line to keep my secret?" Emily's voice was quiet.

"Of course," Micah said.

Emily took a deep breath. Before she could speak, Micah started talking again. "Em, Jared told me about the agreement or whatever you two have going on. But it's not necessary. I told him I'd destroy him if he defiled you in any way. He's not going to out you."

A few tears streaked Emily's cheeks. "That's admirable. I told you that you were brave." She imparted a flimsy smile and shook her head. "But my being with him has nothing to do with that."

"What? I don't understand."

"When Jared came to me, he threatened to tell the school about me and Sam. He made me his stupid offer and I told him no. I told him he could tell the entire school I was gay, but there was no way I was going to go out with him," Emily explained.

"So then why did you?"

"Because, Micah. Then he threatened to do something else." Emily's voice grew angry.

"What?"

Emily looked up at Micah. "He was going to out *you* to the school."

Micah's eyes began to water. "What? How did he know I was gay? I never told him that."

"Well, whatever you talked about in the principal's office gave him enough reason to assume. When he came to me, he convinced me that he knew. He must have been bluffing and he fooled me. I didn't have all the facts. All I knew was that you had just come out to me and that you're figuring out this major thing in your life. I wasn't going to sit back and let him fuck it up for you. I wasn't going to let him humiliate you. So I agreed."

"I can't believe he did that to you."

Emily took Micah's hand and held it tightly. "He's not exactly trustworthy. He played us."

Micah started to cry. "You did that for me?" She smiled sadly. "We sacrificed ourselves for each other?"

"It seems that way." Emily took another deep breath. "Thanks for having my back, Micah," Emily said, and she leaned over. The two of them embraced. Micah closed her eyes and more tears trickled down her face. After a few minutes, Emily pulled back.

"Micah, I'm sorry I didn't come to you sooner. I was just trying to protect you, but I wasn't ready for you to know that. I needed to be sure first that you were happy with Casey; that it wasn't all for nothing. You're still with her so you must be happy. I can rest easy now because I got it right this time."

Micah shook her head. "No."

Two more tears rolled off Emily's cheeks, one from each eye. "What is it?"

Micah opened her mouth to clarify but anguish squelched her response. "Nothing. I…I'm lucky to have someone who looks out for me like you do. I guess my mom was right. I do need a bodyguard."

"What?"

Micah chuckled. "Never mind. It's not important. Em?"

"Yeah?"

"He's expecting you to sleep with him the night of the dance," Micah said, still feeling ill.

Emily nodded. "I figured as much."

"You were going to?" Micah's eyes widened.

"I don't know. Maybe? If that's what it took. It's just sex."

Micah pursed her lips. "What's the difference?"

"Between what?"

"Between 'just sex' and something more?" Micah queried, her chin jutting outward.

"It's all in how you feel about the other person," Emily said earnestly.

"And what is it with Sam?" Micah asked.

Emily shrugged. "Honestly?"

"Yes."

"It's just sex."

Micah's taut jaw relaxed and a tiny sigh of relief escaped. *What was that? She didn't notice, right?*

Emily's eyes twinkled.

She did! Micah immediately tensed back up and began to perspire.

"Why does it matter to you?" Emily asked.

"Uh. Because you're my best friend and I want you to be happy. I think you deserve more than just sex," Micah said, out of breath.

Emily half-smiled. "Thanks." Emily's eyes cast down to the floor. "You know you do, too, right? You deserve more than just sex."

"Oh. Yeah. I know that," Micah floundered. "Anyways so what do we do now?"

"What do you mean?"

"I'm not letting you go through this with Jared anymore. We're in this together and we're taking him down."

Emily smiled. "Alright. Do you have a strategy?"

"Yes! Break up with him!" Micah exclaimed as she stood up.

Emily stood up to meet Micah's eyes. "He'll out us both."

"Who the fuck cares?"

Emily waited for Micah's apology that she usually delivered moments after she swore, but nothing came. "No apology?"

"Emily, I'm being serious. Your happiness is just as important as mine. We're going to get you out of this." Micah looked around. "Where's your phone?"

Emily took her phone out of her pants pocket. "Here. Why?"

"Text him. Tell him you're done with this."

"I can't just text him, Micah. I need to do it in person."

"Is that really the safest idea?" Micah's voice was shrill.

"It's not one of those things you do over a text," Emily said and then her voice softened. "And I have to know if you meant it."

"If I meant what?"

"That you really don't care if he outs us, because he probably will," Emily said, frowning.

"Yes! Obviously I meant it."

Emily's face brightened and she took off towards the door. "I'll be back later!" she said, running down the stairs.

"Emily! Where are you going? Our project? Wait!" Micah yelled.

"Two hours tops!" Emily hollered back. The front door slammed shut.

Micah's breathing became shallow. An acute hammering rippled between her temples. She sat down as the furniture in her room began to whirl, and kneaded her head with her knuckles. Emily's essence circulated through her room. This quelled Micah's anxiety. She got up and found her footing. She went downstairs, picked up the car keys from the counter, and reconciled with her truth.

"Here we go," she said to herself.

Chapter Twenty

Micah parked her mom's car in front of Casey's house with no recollection of actually *driving* there. She walked around to the back of Casey's house and knocked on the door. There was no answer. Micah impatiently knocked again until she heard footsteps approaching. Something eclipsed the peephole and the door opened. Casey's face widened into a big smile when she saw Micah standing on the stoop.

"Hey! I wasn't expecting to see you this soon," Casey said, motioning for Micah to come inside. Casey's eyebrows crinkled. "It's only 11:15. Don't you have to work on your project?"

As Micah slowly entered the house, Casey moved to welcome her with a kiss. Micah deflected Casey's lips so they landed on Micah's cheek.

Casey's smile evaporated.

Micah fixed her eyes on Casey and gently placed her hand on Casey's left shoulder.

"About that. We had to push it back. Emily had something going on." Micah put her hands in her pockets. "Um, can we go talk somewhere?"

Casey looked around the kitchen and then back at Micah. "My dad's at work. We can talk here." She tilted her head. "What's up?"

Micah glanced around the room and nodded. "Okay."

"Look, Micah, if it's about this morning and what I said, I—"

"I don't love you," Micah said softly.

"Micah, forget about it." Casey shrugged. "I don't even know why I said it."

One side of Micah's mouth turned up. She scratched her head. "Casey, did you not mean it?" Micah asked.

Casey looked Micah in the eyes. "Okay, fine. I meant it. But it's not a big deal." Casey shrugged a second time.

Micah stood with her arms open. "Yes, Casey, it *is* a big deal. I can't do this."

"What are you talking about? Do what?" Casey asked. Her voice shook slightly.

Micah closed her eyes and winced. She then looked at Casey. "I can't be with you if you love me, because I don't love you back."

Casey's eyes filled with tears. "But it's okay, Micah. Some people fall in love over time. Just give it time." Casey's voice broke.

Micah's bottom lip began to quiver. She rubbed the back of her own neck.

"Casey, I need you to listen to me. I won't fall in love with you. Not even in time. It's not going to work that way for me. For us," Micah said somberly.

"But you like me?"

"Yes, I do. I like you a lot," Micah said.

"And you find me attractive?"

"Casey, you know I do."

"And we get along?" Casey reached towards Micah.

Micah veered to the side and Casey's arms dropped.

"We do." Micah's lips compressed.

"Then why can't be together?"

"Casey, I'm sorry." Micah crossed her arms gingerly.

"You're sorry? You used me!" Casey accused.

Micah's jaw dropped. "What?"

"You wanted to know what it would be like to be with a girl. I made advances on you, so you decided to experiment with me. This was never real to you! I fucking cared about you. I thought you were different!" Casey shouted. Her face buckled and she began to sob.

Micah reached for her but Casey stepped back.

"Casey, I didn't use you." Micah reigned in her own tears. "I cared about you, too. I CARE about you."

"Then why the hell are you breaking up with me?" Casey blubbered.

"Because. You love me and I don't reciprocate those feelings. It's the right thing to do."

"How do you know your feelings won't change?" Casey asked tenuously.

Micah's face sloped. "I just know."

Casey stepped closer until she was standing right in front of Micah. Casey leaned in slowly to kiss Micah. Micah put her hands on Casey's shoulders to hold her back.

"Don't." Micah spoke in an undertone. "Casey, I really do like you a lot, but..." Micah's eyes grew soft. She bowed her head and shook it.

Casey slapped Micah's hands off her shoulders. "You love someone else, don't you?" Casey said, nodding definitively.

Micah shook her head again. "Casey."

"Tell me the truth, Micah. Is there someone else?" Casey demanded.

"Okay, yes. And I don't think anything will come of it, but I can't be with you if I'm always thinking about her." Micah swallowed.

"You're talking about Emily, aren't you?" Casey asked.

Micah looked down at the floor. She hesitated then looked up. "Yes."

"Argh! I knew it!" Casey's fingers molded into claws. "I should've trusted my gut. The way you look at her." Casey stared at Micah with now empty eyes. "So you're in love with your best friend. How adorable," Casey said caustically.

Micah was immobilized. Her mouth parched. There were no words.

"She'll break your heart, you know."

Micah said nothing and Casey kept talking. "Straight girls always break your heart."

Micah regrouped. "Casey, it still doesn't make it right. If I have feelings for her, then I shouldn't be with you. Do you understand?"

"Let me get this straight. Pun fully intended. You would rather pine after your best friend, who's dating a guy who beats her, so how screwed up is that? Than be with an actual lesbian who wants to be with you? Am I getting this?" Casey's question came out as a maniacal screech and she began to cry again.

"Casey?" Micah's voice was calm.

"What?" Casey seethed.

"Can I hug you?"

Casey didn't answer. Instead, she slumped against the kitchen counter and slid down to the floor. She burrowed her face in her hands and wept. Micah sat beside her. Without permission, she put her arms around Casey and held her while she bawled.

"I'm so so sorry," Micah whispered.

Casey wormed free from Micah's hold on her and began hitting Micah's chest with her fists.

"Don't touch me! I trusted you with my heart and you broke it!"

Casey jumped to her feet and then reached down to grab Micah by her shirt collar. Frightened, Micah quickly got up off the floor.

"Get out! Now. I don't ever want to see you again. EVER!" Casey screamed as she pushed Micah through the doorway.

Micah stood on the back porch facing Casey, who was still inside. They stared at each other.

"I'm sorry you feel that way. But I really do care about you," Micah said as she started to cry, too.

"But you don't love me."

"No, I don't," Micah said quietly.

"Go home, Micah. Go home to your safe crushes on straight girls so that no one will ever find out who you really are!"

Micah nodded. She did what she was told and walked away.

Micah parked the car in its rightful spot in the driveway and burst into the house through the kitchen. She hurled the door shut and gripped the steel knob. Her eyes became glassy and then overflowed. She went to exhale but it came out as a scream. With fiery eyes, she went over to the table and picked up a neglected coffee mug. She hurtled it against the wall. She watched it shatter into small pieces. Ah! It was her father's favorite mug! Micah's lungs strived for oxygen. She tumbled to the floor. *Superglue. I can put it back together.* Tears impaired her vision as she collected the pieces of porcelain.

"Shit!" A sharp pain shot through her right palm, which began to ooze blood. She drudged over to the sink, took a dishrag out of the drawer, and wove it securely around her hand. Blotches of maroon saturated the cloth. The gash was deep. In a trance, she started for the medicine cabinet to retrieve some antiseptic, some gauze, and some tape. Emily entered the front hall, interrupting her.

"You really should lock this," Emily said, pointing to the door. She stopped at the sight of the red towel. Emily locked the door behind her and ran over to Micah.

"What did you do?" Emily asked.

"It's just a cut. I broke something and I went to clean it up."

"Let me see it," Emily said, slowly taking Micah's severed hand into her own. Emily carefully unraveled the sopping cloth and looked closely at the laceration. "It's deep."

"Gee, ya think?" Micah said.

Emily rolled her eyes. "You might need stitches."

"I'm fine. There's stuff in the bathroom I can put on it," Micah said, heading up the stairs. Emily followed close behind.

In the bathroom, Micah took the first aid kid out of the cabinet, and then sat on the edge of the tub. She handed the necessary items to Emily.

"Help?"

Emily knelt in front of Micah and began cleaning out the cut cautiously.

"Where were you?" Emily asked, her eyes on Micah's hand.

"I went for a drive."

"I called you."

"I had my phone off," Micah explained.

Emily sighed. "Are you mad at me?"

"No. But next time you run out of my house like that, some kind of explanation would be nice," Micah said. Her voice cracked.

Emily looked up at Micah. "I took care of everything, so don't worry."

"What does that even mean?" Micah asked.

"I caught up with Jared in the gym. I knew he had basketball practice this morning. I told him that I wasn't going to date him anymore, and that he could take his threats and suck on them."

Micah wrinkled her brow. "What did he say?"

Emily let out a small laugh. "He told me to go fuck myself. I told him that sounded much more pleasant than him fucking me."

Emily finished with Micah's butchered hand. "Okay, you're one hundred percent sterilized."

"Thanks," Micah said.

"Want me to wrap it up?"

"Yes, please."

"You really despise your right hand, don't you?" Emily wisecracked. "I bet Jared's nose does, too."

"I guess so," Micah mumbled.

Emily coughed a little. "I, uh, I also went to go see Sam."

Micah's poker face flopped. "Oh?"

"I told her we had to stop, you know, messing around," Emily said.

Micah tinkered with the fringe of mesh sheathing her wound. "Why?"

"I needed a clean slate. I thought about what you said. I do deserve more."

Micah smiled. "That's good, Em. How'd she take it?"

"She's fine. She'll find someone else."

Micah raised her eyebrows.

Emily chuckled. "Don't ask."

Emily stood up and reached out her hand to assist Micah in getting off the tub. Micah accepted.

"Em?"

"Yeah?"

Micah started to weep. "I'm so tired." Emily frowned and wrapped her arms around Micah.

"Shh. I got you," Emily kept whispering.

Chapter Twenty-One

When Micah woke up, she was on her own bed. Disoriented, she browsed the room and spied Emily sitting at the desk typing. Micah's hand throbbed.

"Ahh!" she squeaked.

Emily looked up at Micah. "Are you suffering over there or what?"

Micah stuck her tongue out at Emily. "Don't be snarky with me. I'm fragile."

Emily wrestled to keep her mouth staid, but the ridges crimped up. "Sure you are." She indicated to the bottle of water on Micah's nightstand. "You should drink something."

Micah sat up and went for the beverage.

"Careful. The cap's loose," Emily warned. "I didn't want you to have to toil with it since you're so frail and all." Emily giggled.

"Ha. Ha." Micah held up the bottle as if to suggest a toast, and took a long sip of the water. "Thanks," she said when she was done. "How long was I out for?"

Emily looked at the clock. "You sort of cried yourself to sleep. I would say three hours or so."

Micah shook her head. "I'm sorry."

"Don't be, but I don't think you can fix it," Emily said.

"Fix what?"

"Your dad's mug. When I went to get you some water, I saw it scattered all over the kitchen. I picked up all the pieces I could find, but it's definitely beyond repair."

Micah stared down into the transparent liquid. "You didn't have to do that."

Emily got up and moved over to the bed. She sat next to Micah.

"I know." Emily took the bottle from Micah's hand and put it back on the nightstand. "Do you want to talk about it?"

Micah shrugged. "I was upset. I threw it. I wasn't thinking."

Emily put her arm around Micah. "It's okay. I'm sure he'll forgive you."

Micah sighed. "We still have to work on that stupid project."

"I already wrote, oh I don't know, ten pages of it," Emily said smugly.

Micah's eyes lit up. "Seriously?"

"Yup."

Micah put her left hand on Emily's leg and squeezed it. "You're the best!"

Emily grinned. "I know."

Micah stood up and steadied herself. "So do you want to keep working on it?"

Emily groaned. "I suppose we don't really have a choice."

"I can write the other half tomorrow?" Micah suggested.

"Or I could help you. We're a team, remember?"

Micah smiled. "Right."

Micah walked over to her desk and reviewed the printed pages of what Emily had written so far. After a few minutes, she looked up at Emily, who had been watching her read.

"It's great!" Micah professed.

"Thanks," Emily said. She glanced pointedly at the empty space on Micah's desk. "I see you took down our picture."

Micah opened up her desk drawer, pulled out the picture, and placed it back on her desk. "Look! All better."

Emily smiled sadly. "I feel like we have so much catching up to do, like I've missed out on part of your life."

"Yeah." Micah nodded. "I feel that way, too."

"So, does Casey want you to go to the dance with her?" Emily's voice quavered.

Micah shook her head. "No."

"Why not?"

Micah held up her swathed extremity. "Can I take this off now? It's itchy."

"It might get infected."

"Well, I'll take my chances."

"Fine," Emily griped. "Come here."

Micah sidled over to Emily, who meticulously detached the dressing. "There, but you can't blame me if you get gangrene."

Micah gleamed. "Thank you!"

"Yeah. Yeah. Stop trying to dodge my question."

"What question?" Micah asked.

"The dance. Why aren't you going with Casey?"

Tell her! "Uh. Because it's probably gonna be lame and I can't dance anyway."

"Yes, you can," Emily said.

"No. We both know I can't."

Emily stood up and walked towards her bag. She pulled out a CD and made her way over to Micah's stereo. She put the disc inside and pressed "play." A woman began crooning along with the mellow strumming of a guitar.

"What is this?" Micah asked.

Emily flushed. "It's a mix CD. I made it for you a few months ago, knowing you'd never get an MP3 player." She smiled a little.

Micah smiled back. "Why did it take you until now to give it to me?"

"I don't know." Emily shrugged and then held out her hand to Micah. "May I?"

Micah nervously placed her hand in Emily's. Emily drew Micah in closer.

"Now, you put your arm here," Emily instructed, putting Micah's arm around her neck. "And I put my hand on your waist like this." Emily gently positioned her hand on Micah's side. A wave of electricity shot through Micah.

"Now, just follow my lead. When I step back, you step back with me. Kind of feel along with what I'm doing with my body," Emily explained. They began dancing. In a swelter, Micah melted into Emily's arms. Emily's cheek suddenly pressed against Micah's.

"See? You know what you're doing," Emily whispered.

Micah pulled away and darted over to the CD player to turn off the music. She looked back at Emily, whose face had whitened.

"I can't," Micah spluttered.

"Micah, I'm sorry. I wasn't trying…you're my best friend and I…," Emily stammered. Micah walked over to Emily and put her hands on Emily's shoulders. Emily fell silent.

"Relax. It's just…there's something I have to tell you."

"I didn't mean to, Micah."

"No, you didn't do anything wrong. I'm not with Casey anymore. I went to her house when you left. I had to end it."

"What? Why?"

Micah smiled and moved her left hand up to Emily's cheek. "Because my heart belongs to someone else." Her voice was velvety.

Emily swallowed hard. "Micah, are you telling me…"

"Emily, you're the one I want to be with." Micah smiled as she spoke.

"This will change everything. Our friendship…," Emily cautioned.

"I know," Micah said, drawing Emily's face closer.

As they stared into each other's eyes, a tear rolled off Emily's cheek.

"Why are you crying?" Micah asked.

"Because I love you," Emily answered.

Micah wiped the tear away with her thumb and smiled sideways.

"I love you, too." Micah's words lingered in the air for a moment and then she slowly brushed her lips against Emily's. Gradually, Emily's lips parted and the warmth of her breath engrossed Micah. Micah opened her mouth and their tongues touched one another's. Emily placed one of her hands on Micah's waist and the other around the back of Micah's neck as the kiss grew deeper.

Emily's lips began to trail across Micah's neck, causing her to shiver.

"Emily," Micah uttered breathlessly.

Emily looked up at Micah. "Do you want me to stop?" Emily asked, trying to catch her breath as well.

Micah grinned and ran her fingers across Emily's face. It felt soft and oddly familiar. It felt like home.

"No." Micah laughed a little and pulled Emily in for another kiss. Their kisses became more passionate, each of them trying to devour the other. Micah gently pushed Emily onto the bed. Emily shot Micah a look of surprise, and then laughed. Emily's hazel eyes sparkled like nothing Micah had ever seen before.

Micah perched in Emily's lap on top of her legs. Emily sat up to continue kissing Micah. Emily pulled Micah's shirt off slowly and tossed it onto the floor. Emily's tongue ran along Micah's collarbone, her chest, the edge of her bra, and her stomach. Emily held herself up by holding onto Micah's back. Micah reached around to grab ahold of Emily's wrists, raising Emily's arms up. She took Emily's top off and then she eased Emily onto her back. Micah lay on top of her and quivered in delight when their bodies connected.

Micah's hands moved leisurely across Emily's body to ensure that she touched every piece of Emily. Micah took off Emily's bra and let her tongue explore Emily's breasts. Emily let out a small moan and unhooked Micah's bra, letting it spill off her shoulders.

Emily cupped Micah's breasts in her hands and massaged them gently. Micah's head tilted back when Emily slightly increased pressure. Micah then leaned forward, and with her tongue drew a line from Emily's chest down to her navel and around Emily's belly button ring.

Micah looked up at Emily and began to slide Emily's pants off. Emily put her hands on Micah's cheeks. Emily pulled Micah back up to kiss her on the mouth, all the while unbuttoning Micah's jeans. She gave them a light tug so that they fell below Micah's hips. Micah used one of her own hands to assist Emily in removing the pants.

Micah stopped to glance down at their bodies writhing together. She reverted her eyes to Emily's face and smiled. Emily smiled back and then pressed her lips hard against Micah's. Micah indulged Emily in this kiss for a moment and then ran her hand over Emily's underwear. Micah gasped when she felt how wet they were. Before Micah had a chance, Emily was pulling down her own underwear with an unfiltered urgency. Once Emily had accomplished this task, she took off Micah's as well.

Micah started kissing Emily's naked body. Her hands caressed the back of Emily's thighs as her tongue grazed between them, delicately at first but then with more vigor. Everything about Emily was smooth against Micah's mouth. Emily gasped for air and then drew

Micah back up to her. Emily wiped Micah's mouth with her hand. Micah smiled.

"You didn't have to do that," Emily whispered before engaging Micah in another fervid kiss. Micah waited for a break in the kiss.

"I know. I wanted to," Micah rasped. With finesse, Emily grabbed Micah by the shoulders and flipped her onto her back. Emily was now on top. Micah laughed.

"What are you doing? I'm not done," Micah playfully protested.

Emily slid her body across Micah's, moving downward. Just like in Micah's dream, she heard herself moan as Emily's tongue slipped inside of her. Micah did not attempt to interrupt Emily. Micah's entire body ignited as Emily's fingers replaced her tongue without missing a beat. Emily, keeping her fingers between Micah's thighs, moved herself back up so that her body was parallel to Micah's. Micah opened her eyes to see Emily, who was smiling down at her. Emily did not need to tell Micah to relax. She *was* relaxed. Something began to ache inside Micah and her body trembled.

"Emily?" Micah barely whispered. Emily kept her fingers moving at the same rhythm.

"I'm right here," she whispered back, and then she felt Micah's whole body seize up beneath her.

Micah suddenly felt what she could only describe as an intense release where the ache had been just moments ago. Without control of her own vocal chords, she groaned in pleasure. Emily's fingers began to move at a slower pace before coming to a halt. Micah opened her eyes again. Emily had beads of sweat across her forehead. She was exquisite and Micah savored her beauty. Micah began to cry, wrapping her arms around Emily.

Emily buried her face in Micah's neck. "Shh."

Micah started to laugh at her own reaction. "Oh my god, I don't even know why I'm crying!"

Emily kissed Micah's cheek. "It happens sometimes when it's over."

"Wow," Micah said.

Emily laughed. "Right?"

Micah bit her bottom lip and smiled, rolling herself on top of Emily.

"Hey, what are you doing? Rest for a second!" Emily was still laughing.

Micah shook her head. "No way." Micah began kissing Emily again as her hands slithered down the sides of Emily's body.

"Hey, hey. What about your hand?"

"Lucky for you, I'm a lefty," Micah whispered. Emily's head fell back onto the pillow. She closed her eyes tightly as Micah's fingers eagerly entered her body. Emily's breathing became heavy. Her legs spread further apart. From the inside out, Micah glided over Emily's source of arousal. This went on for several minutes until

Emily's body tightened around Micah's hand. Emily let out a moan, but it wasn't just a noise. It was Micah's name. Then all of Emily's muscles slowly relaxed.

"You," Emily said, grinning up at Micah.

Micah kissed her on the forehead. "Hi."

The room was still and their eyes fixed on one another.

"What just happened?" Micah asked, a smile playing across her lips.

Emily beamed. "We totally just took our relationship to the next level. Micah?"

"Yeah?"

"*That* was more than 'just sex,'" Emily said in a throaty voice with lustering eyes.

"I know." Micah laughed, almost giddy, and wrapped her body around Emily's. The two girls lay there, in the comfort of one another's arms, tangled together as if they were one. Micah rested her head on Emily's chest. She closed her eyes as she listened to Emily's heartbeat, a sound more wonderful than anything she had ever heard.

"And, Micah?"

"Yeah?" Micah asked without looking up.

"In case you're wondering, this is what it feels like when your mind and your body *aren't* betraying each other," Emily whispered.

Micah smiled and intertwined her fingers with Emily's to let her know that she understood.

Chapter Twenty-Two

"You know we've been lying here for like an hour?" Micah asked, looking behind her at the clock.

Emily was on her side, resting her head on her arm. She twisted Micah's necklace around her finger, and then came closer to kiss Micah's bare shoulder.

"I'm having fun," Emily said through a smile.

"Me too, but we can't just stay in bed staring at each other all day."

"I'm afraid to look away," Emily said softly.

"Why's that?"

"What if I get out of this bed and reality comes crashing down and you change your mind?"

Micah kissed Emily longingly until they were both panting. Micah licked her lips.

"Or not." Emily laughed lightly while catching her breath.

"Can I tell you something that might assuage your fears?" Micah asked.

Emily smiled. "You can try."

Micah's cheeks flared. "I, um, kept dreaming about you."

"Okay. You're in my dreams sometimes, too."

Micah laughed. "In *your* dreams, we're both superheroes."

"So? You're still in them," Emily said, smirking.

"But in my dreams, we were being, um, intimate."

Emily grinned. "Oh? How was I?"

Micah picked up the pillow she was leaning on and went to hit Emily with it. Emily skillfully caught the pillow mid-air and got on top of Micah.

"Nice try. We've been pillow fighting since grade school. You should know by now that you can't win."

"Maybe I just let you win," Micah said, looking up at Emily.

"I think you're lying."

"Well, I am."

Emily smiled. "So tell me more about these dreams."

"They felt so real," Micah said. She closed her eyes, trying to remember all of the details. Emily lowered her body on top of Micah's. Micah opened her eyes, distracted, and put each of her hands on Emily's torso.

"You have a great body," Micah said.

"So do you." Emily smiled. "I've been admiring it for a few years now."

"Oh really?"

Emily sucked her teeth. "Sorry. I couldn't help it."

Micah laughed. "It's okay. But the thing about the dreams is that—"

"Yes, the dreams," Emily said. She started to kiss Micah's neck.

"I can't concentrate when you do that," Micah said, her insides pulsating.

"Do what?" Emily asked in an innocent tone, her lips still sweeping Micah's skin.

Micah started tickling Emily's stomach. Emily shrieked and sat back up, defensively covering her abdomen with her arms.

"That was a cheap shot!"

"Listen to me, okay?"

"Okay, I'm listening."

"So once the dreams started, it was hard to look at you the same way. And I couldn't stop thinking about them. I got this feeling and I knew. I tried to fight it, but I…"

Emily half-smiled. "Why did you try to fight it?"

"Because it was before I even knew you liked me. I was freaking out. I was having sex dreams about my best friend who I thought was straight!" Micah spewed. "But all this time, you…"

"I was totally gay for you." Emily laughed. "I almost died when you told me your mom thought we were dating."

Micah started to laugh too. "This is crazy."

"Is it?"

Micah stared up at Emily, their eyes searching each other's faces.

"Your eyes. They're so blue. They change, like when you laugh or cry or when you're excited." Emily spoke in a quiet manner. "For years they've been enticing me, and I can't believe that they're on me now."

Micah inhaled each syllable.

"Emily, I know that I told you that I loved you, but"—Micah looked away and over at the picture of the two of them on her desk. She was sure.—"I'm *in* love with you."

Emily lifted Micah's body up so that Micah was sitting in front of her. She stared at Micah momentarily before speaking.

"I'm in love with you, too." Then she kissed Micah feverishly. Micah returned the kiss and this exchange went on for some time. Micah slowed the kiss down and pecked Emily on the lips. She started to laugh.

"If you keep kissing me like that, we're never going to finish our project."

Emily smiled. "So what? Failing the class is a miniscule price to pay."

Micah pointed at Emily. "We're not going to fail."

"Are you trying to tell me that we have to get dressed?" Emily pouted.

"Well, I don't think we'll be able to focus if we're naked on my bed."

Emily looked Micah up and down. "Agreed."

Micah reached down and grabbed their shirts off the floor. She struggled getting her arms through the sleeves of hers. Emily helped her put on the shirt. She smiled at Micah and Micah kissed Emily's cheek.

"Okay, so we'll have dinner, finish our project, and then we can use our free time to…" Micah's head descended.

"To what?" Emily teased knowingly.

Micah glanced back up at Emily and winked. Then she kissed Emily on the cheek.

Emily shook her head. "Wow."

"What?"

"Nothing," Emily said.

"No. What?"

Emily looked right at Micah. "I can't believe you just winked at me! Micah, you're…"

"I'm what?" Micah paused. "I know. That was weird, right? I shouldn't have winked at you." Micah shook her head.

"No! No, I liked it. It was sexy," Emily said, turning her gaze away.

"Are you blushing?"

"Me? Never," Emily said, turning back to Micah.

Micah planted a light kiss on Emily's lips. "You're not too bad yourself."

"Why, thank you." Emily smiled and agilely got dressed without leaving the bed. Then she mumbled, "You know I cried?"

Micah put her hand over Emily's and tilted her head.

Emily continued, "The day you came out to me and told me you liked Casey, I went home and I cried."

"I'm sorry."

"No, don't be sorry. You're here now and I can't believe how perfect it is."

Micah smiled. "Me either." She got off the bed to put her jeans on. "But, Emily?"

"Yeah?"

"What happens when your parents find out?"

Emily let out a long sigh. "Who knows?"

Micah squeezed her hand. "We'll get through it. I'm not letting you do this alone."

"Let's not worry about it." Emily stood up and started towards the bedroom door. "Come on. I'll make you pancakes."

Micah followed her to the kitchen as if they were children again racing towards the playground, feeling as happy in her heart now as she did then.

"Done!" Micah cheered, dropping a textbook to the floor. They had been working on their project for several hours after eating.

Emily looked up from the pages that had already been typed. "Seriously? We're finished?"

"Seriously."

"Nice!" Emily knelt up to level herself with Micah, who was sitting on her desk chair. Emily raised her hand and they high-fived each other.

"Crushed it!" Micah said.

"So now what?" Emily's eyes flickered as she pulled Micah to the floor. Micah complied. As Emily lay back down, Micah sat on top of her.

"Well, what do you want to do?" Micah asked, her face lucent.

Emily put both of her hands behind her head and stared up at Micah.

"What are you doing?" Micah asked suspiciously.

"Staring at you. What does it look like I'm doing?"

"Staring contest!" Micah declared.

"I don't know why you keep challenging me to things you always lose at," Emily said, sitting up.

"I might win."

"Okay. And what do you want if you win?" Emily asked.

Micah slowly began to smile, as she had given her answer a lot of thought. "I want a favor."

"What's the favor?" Emily asked, wary.

"That's the best part. I can redeem my favor at any time so I don't need to tell you." Micah folded her arms across her chest.

Emily scoffed. "*If* you should win, I'll grant you a favor."

"What do you want if you win?"

"I already got what I wanted so I'm just humoring you," Emily said.

"Fine then. Are you ready?" Micah asked. She compacted her facial muscles.

"Ready," Emily said, half of her mouth still curled up in a smile.

"Go."

The two girls stared at one another intensely. Micah began submitting to her suppressed laughter, when suddenly Emily started to shake violently. Micah jumped up so that she could lay next to Emily and comfort her, but Emily's arms and legs were flailing all over the place. Emily was gasping for air. Her eyes began to roll in the back of her head and her lips turned blue.

"Emily!" Micah yelled. She watched Emily's body suddenly stop moving. She placed her hand against Emily's cheek, but Emily was still. Micah pressed her head up to Emily's chest and couldn't hear anything.

"Emily!" she screamed. "Emily, don't!" Her eyes filled with tears as she frantically searched for her phone under all the papers on her desk. She found the phone and dialed 911.

"911, Operator. What is your emergency?"

Micah was crying as she knelt back down on the floor and held Emily's hand.

"My friend, she's...she was convulsing and now she's not breathing...I don't think she's breathing! I can't tell...please help her!"

Chapter Twenty-Three

Micah sat curled up in a hospital waiting room chair with Emily's sweatshirt wrapped around her. She kept replaying the last few minutes before Emily was taken away in an ambulance. She closed her eyes, hoping that when she opened them, she would be back in her bedroom with Emily sleeping soundly by her side.

She heard familiar voices and turned around. It was Emily's parents. Micah got out of her seat.

"Mr. and Mrs. Mathis, over here," Micah said, waving to them. Emily's parents made their way towards Micah.

"What the hell happened?" Emily's father roared.

"Calm yourself down," Emily's mother snapped back.

Both Mr. and Mrs. Mathis stared at Micah. Their eyes were red. Their faces were white.

Micah exhaled.

"Um, the emergency response team said they think she had a seizure. The doctors won't tell me anything because I'm not family." Micah paused. "She was fine and then all of a sudden, she…" Micah's eyes watered again.

"That's all you can tell us?" Mr. Mathis's voice echoed throughout the room.

"Will you stop your yammering? She told us all she knows!" Mrs. Mathis glared at her husband, and then put her arm on Micah's shoulder. "He's worried, that's all. The doctors know we're here now, so maybe we can all wait together?"

Micah nodded and the three of them sat down in silence for a few minutes. The smell of Mr. Mathis's cologne was potent. Mrs. Mathis kept spinning her wedding ring around her finger.

A recognizable voice breached the awkward quiet. "Micah!"

Micah turned around and her parents were there. Micah ran over to them, Emily's sweatshirt gripped in her hand. She reached her parents and they swarmed together. Micah began sobbing.

"I'm sorry I called you," Micah cried.

"Shh, sweetie. It's okay. We're glad you called. What happened? Is Emily okay?" Micah's mom asked.

Micah looked up at the concerned expressions of her parents. "They think it was a seizure. That's all I know."

Mr. Williams wrapped his arm around Micah and brought her over to sit down on a chair. He sat beside her.

"Tell me what happened."

Micah looked up at her dad, over at her mom who was sitting on the other side of her, and then back at her dad.

"We were just hanging out and she started shaking and she couldn't breathe and then she just stopped moving! They wouldn't let me ride in the back of the ambulance to hold her hand." Micah held up her cut hand. "And I broke your favorite mug, Dad! I'm sorry!" The tears were chapping Micah's cheeks.

Mr. Williams rubbed Micah's head. "It's okay. It was old. Its time had come," he consoled.

"Deep breaths. Let's calm down," Mrs. Williams soothed, carefully inspecting Micah's hand.

"Mom," Micah whispered, looking sadly up at her mother.

"Yes?"

"She *has* to be alright. I love her."

Micah's mom gave her a stoic smile. "I know you do."

Micah gaped, still sniveling. "You know?"

Her mom handed her a tissue, nodding. "Honey, a mother always knows."

Micah let out a partial laugh of disbelief. She shook her head. "Mom, I'm scared."

"She'll be okay. She's strong, just like you."

"Excuse me?" Micah and her parents looked up to see Emily's parents standing there, staring down at them.

"I'm sorry?" Mrs. Williams said, protectively tightening her arm around Micah.

"Did you just say you *loved* my daughter? Are you and my daughter...is *my* daughter...," Mr. Mathis's gruff voice blundered as he pointed directly at Micah.

Micah's dad stood up. "Look, Mr. Mathis, we're all worried. How about we just sit down and try to relax and see what the doctor says?"

Mr. Mathis shook his head. Neither his eyes nor his finger had budged. "You and Emily?" His tone was menacing. "Answer me!"

Micah tried to pull out of her mother's grasp, but Mrs. Williams wouldn't let go.

"Don't, Micah. This isn't your battle," she whispered harshly. Her compassionate eyes morphed into daggers as they bore into Emily's dad.

"Mr. Mathis, right now your daughter is lying in a hospital bed and none of us knows why. I suggest you get your priorities straightened out before you start attacking my daughter. Or yours for that matter," Micah's mom reprimanded.

Mrs. Mathis gave Mrs. Williams a conspiring nod of approval. "Let's go sit down," Emily's mother said, pulling Mr. Mathis to the other side of the waiting room.

Mr. and Mrs. Williams were mute. Micah turned to the clock above the registration desk. Her eyes burned, making the numbers fuzzy. She'd already been waiting over three hours. Micah rested her head against her mother's shoulder. She began to doze off, but a baritone sound diverted her attention.

"Mr. and Mrs. Mathis?" the doctor pronounced.

Emily's parents walked over to the doctor. His lips moved, but Micah couldn't read them from across the room. When the doctor was finished, Mr. and Mrs. Mathis hugged one another, and then looked back at Micah.

"She's asking for you," Mrs. Mathis said. "Come on." She motioned for Micah to accompany them to Emily's room. Micah glanced over at her own mother, who nudged her to go.

Emily's parents and Micah followed the doctor to Emily's hospital room.

Before the doctor opened the door, he addressed Emily's parents. "Were you aware that your daughter came to the ER a few weeks ago? She had been in a fight."

Mrs. Mathis's mouth dropped. "What?" She crossed her arms. "Emily told us she was in a fight, but she didn't say that she came to the hospital. She said that the fight was at school and that the school nurse stitched her up." Emily's mom began to cry. "I thought it was peculiar that the school never contacted me, but I wasn't about to question her. I didn't want to be *that* prying mother. She resents me enough as it is."

"Well," the doctor continued, "according to our records, during that fight Emily hit her head on the pavement."

Emily's father took a sharp intake of air.

The doctor went on, "The nurse recommended that she stay for observation to make sure she didn't suffer a concussion, but she signed herself out against medical advice."

"For Christ's sake!" Emily's dad muttered.

"Did you know about this, Micah?" Mrs. Mathis asked.

"No," Micah lied. "But I know she was afraid to tell you guys about coming to the hospital."

"Why?" Mrs. Mathis asked, befuddled.

"Because. She says you guys fight a lot and she's afraid. She doesn't know if you'll support her or not." *There! It had to be said. Emily will understand, won't she?*

Emily's parents paled. They looked at each other, at the doctor, and then at Micah. "She's our daughter! We love her no matter what," Emily's dad said firmly, "even if she's…well, we still love her."

"I don't think she knows that," Micah said, her voice steady.

The doctor started talking again. "Emily suffered from what we call a post traumatic seizure, based on our findings from the CT scan. You see, it appears that she did in fact get a concussion from that fall. The residual effect of the head injury caused her to have a seizure. It's not uncommon. We gave her a dose of an anti-convulsant and a sedative, because she wouldn't relax enough for us to inject the intravenous rehydration tube. She's still a little confused, and she'll be sore for a few days, but otherwise she should be fine."

"Thank you, Doctor," Mr. Mathis said, shaking the doctor's hand. They watched the doctor walk away, his white coat fading into the hospital walls.

Micah looked at Emily's parents. "I'll wait out here."

Mr. and Mrs. Mathis stared at each other for a moment and then went into Emily's room. Micah checked her cell phone. It was a little after 8 p.m. She began pacing the hallways. Twenty-three minutes later, Emily's parents emerged from the room. They came towards Micah.

"She's asking for you," Mrs. Mathis said. "She's insistent."

Micah smiled. "Okay." She walked over to the door and knocked on it. "Delivery," Micah joked as she opened the door all the way.

Emily was lying on the hospital bed, an IV hooked up to her hand and tubes up her nostrils. Micah took a deep breath. Emily gave her a small smile.

"Finally! I placed that order like forty minutes ago." Emily motioned for Micah to come closer.

Micah smiled and moved over to Emily's bed.

"Sit," Emily said, patting the extra room on her bed. Micah sat down and took Emily's hand.

"How are you?" Micah asked. "The doctor said you were still confused."

"A little. Things are kinda foggy. I remember looking at you, and then I woke up and I was here."

"We were having a staring contest, and then"—Micah swallowed her urge to cry—"you started shaking and I couldn't hear your heart beat. I thought…"

"Hey, hey. I'm not going anywhere. Are you kidding me? Now that I've got the girl, you think they're going to write me out of the story?" Emily asked, laughing lightly. "Damn it, you kicked my ass in that contest."

Micah smiled. "I'm so crazy about you. Don't ever scare me like that again."

"You got it. Lay with me?" Emily requested.

Micah nodded and stretched out next to Emily. She rested her head on Emily's shoulder and put one of her arms across Emily's stomach. Emily placed her hand on Micah's arm.

"Does it hurt?" Micah asked.

"A little."

"I heard you were asking for me."

"Well, when I asked for Hot Megan from The Bean, they told me she was on call so I had to settle for you." Emily chuckled.

Micah looked up at her. "You're quite the comedian on all those drugs, huh?"

"Hey, girl's gotta have a sense of humor."

Micah raised her eyebrows at Emily. "So I'm your number two, huh? Thanks a lot."

"You know you're my number one! You do know that, right?" Emily asked.

"I know. You're mine, too. My number one." Micah exhaled. "Emily, will you be my girlfriend?"

"Are *you* asking *me* out?" Emily was smiling, the light returning to her eyes.

"Yes."

"While we're in the hospital?"

"Yes."

"Even with these sexy tubes hanging out of my nose?"

"Especially because of that," Micah said. She kissed Emily's cheek. "When I wake up tomorrow, I want to know you're mine."

"Possessive much?" Emily laughed.

"Em, I'm serious. Will you go out with me? Will you be my girlfriend?"

"Yes, I'll be your girlfriend," Emily replied and then shook her head.

"Why do you look disappointed?"

"Because, Micah. *I* wanted to ask *you*. I can't believe you beat me to it," Emily complained.

"Well excuse me, oh chivalrous one. Look at it as me taking advantage of your head injury."

Emily smiled. "Okay, I can handle that."

Micah rested her head back down on Emily. She watched Emily's chest rise and fall. She smiled to herself. She had seen and felt the flesh under Emily's hospital gown. *You're in the hospital! Virtuous thoughts only.*

"What are you thinking about?" Emily asked.

"Oh, um. I'm just really glad we're both going to State together next year."

"Such a bad liar, but we *would* have a fun time as roommates," Emily said.

Micah closed her eyes. "How do you know when I'm lying?"

"You don't answer me right away. You have these little hesitations. Sometimes it's with your eyes, sometimes your words, but I can usually tell."

Emily's heart monitor beeped. It was the only sound in the room for the next few minutes.

"My parents told me they overheard you talking to your parents," Emily started. "I don't know what they heard, but they asked me if we were together."

"Then what?" Micah asked. *Don't panic.*

"I told them we were. I figured there was no safer place to tell them than in a hospital. Am I right?" Emily said, laughing a little.

Micah waited for Emily to continue. She didn't look up.

"They had the strangest reaction. Do you know what they said?" Emily asked.

"What?"

"They told me that they loved me because I was their daughter, and they don't want me to be afraid to tell them the truth. Then they apologized for, like, everything," Emily said.

Micah looked up at Emily. "That's great!"

"I know you had a part in this."

Micah smiled and shrugged. "Maybe they needed to hear how scared their daughter was. You certainly weren't going to tell them." Micah rested her head again.

"You're always looking out for me," Emily slurred. The sedatives were taking effect.

"We look out for each other."

"This was the best weekend," Emily mumbled. Micah looked around the hospital room and then at Emily. Her eyes were shut.

"Yeah, who could ask for anything more?" Micah said with a hint of sarcasm in her tone.

"You were so pretty. In your little blue, striped shirt on the first day of first grade," Emily said as if she were talking in her sleep. "I watched you on the swings. I wanted to play with you. I should've known then."

"Shh. Get some sleep," Micah said, brushing a few hairs off Emily's forehead before she kissed it. She listened for the change in Emily's breathing. When she knew for sure that Emily was asleep, Micah lay back down next to her.

Emily remembered that? Micah had hated that shirt and begged her mom to let her wear something else that day. Emily had had on overalls and Micah was jealous of her. Micah had been watching her, too.

"Good night, Emily," she whispered.

Something prodded Micah's arm. She opened her eyes and looked up. Her mother was there.

"Sweetie, your father and I have to go." Mrs. Williams's voice was soft.

Micah sat up slowly, turned back to look at Emily, and then faced her mom. "What time is it?"

"It's eleven. We have to head back to the Cape. When you called, we literally ran out of the cottage. We realized on the way here that we didn't lock it up. It might be a good idea for you to go home, too," her mother said.

"I want to stay."

"You should check with Emily's parents. If they ask you to leave, don't argue with them."

"She can stay," a voice said from the doorway.

Micah and her mother looked over to see Mrs. Mathis standing there.

"We're heading out. They want to keep her overnight for observation. I'm sure she'd want you to stay," Emily's mother said.

"Really?" Micah asked Mrs. Mathis.

Mrs. Mathis smiled. "I don't see why not."

Micah's mom looked at Mrs. Mathis. "Thank you."

Mrs. Mathis nodded. "It's no problem."

Mrs. Williams bent over and kissed Micah on the top of her head. "I love you. We'll see you tomorrow night. Are you sure you'll be okay here?"

Micah nodded. "I'm sure."

"See you soon then. I love you."

"I love you, too, Mom," Micah said. Her mom left the room, stopping on the way out to put her arm on Mrs. Mathis briefly. Then she was gone.

Mrs. Mathis came into the room and pulled a chair up next to Emily's bed. Micah began to get up.

"Stay there," Emily's mom requested.

Micah didn't move a muscle.

"You make her happy," Mrs. Mathis started. "Ever since you were little, she always wanted to be around you. She never stopped wanting to be around you." Mrs. Mathis shook her head. Her eyes had the same almond shape as Emily's. The resemblance was striking. "I thought it was a phase. I thought that eventually things would change, but she smiled so much whenever she talked about you."

"I'm not sure what to…I'm sorry?" Micah offered.

"Don't be sorry. Your mother and I had a long talk in the waiting room. I know she cares about Emily, and I see now how much you do, too." There was a silence. "A week or so ago, I went into Emily's room to put her laundry on her bed. Her journal was there. I knew I shouldn't, but I did. She hadn't been acting like herself after that fight and she wouldn't talk to me. I'm her mother. I worry about her and I wanted to know what was going on, but I couldn't get her to tell me anything. I opened it and I read it. Just one page. That's all I needed and I had the answers. I know that if I can show her that I accept…this…, then maybe she'll forgive me for all the times I failed her as a mother." Mrs. Mathis covered her mouth with her hand as she began to cry.

Micah waited.

Mrs. Mathis collected herself. "Micah, I trust you." She stood up.

Micah nodded.

"I'll see you two in the morning," Mrs. Mathis said. She touched Emily's hand and left.

Once the clacking of Mrs. Mathis's heels desisted, Micah let out a breath that she wasn't aware she had been holding. Her weary body collapsed next to Emily's.

Micah closed her eyes. Since the day they met, Micah never wanted to stop being around Emily either. Micah smiled and drifted off into a deep sleep.

Chapter Twenty-Four

The sound of sirens woke Micah up.

"Hey," Emily said. "Good morning."

Micah looked around and realized where she was. She smiled at Emily. "Good morning. How long have you been up?"

"About forty-five minutes. I liked watching you sleep."

"Why didn't you wake me?"

"You looked peaceful." Emily leaned over to kiss Micah.

"Em, my breath is probably kicking," Micah warned.

"And you think that's going to stop me?" Emily's lips lightly swept across Micah's.

"Mmm. It *is* a good morning."

Emily smiled. "It sure is."

Micah sat up. "What time is your mom coming?"

"She said she'd be here around nine. It's like 9:03 now, so I guess anytime soon."

Micah got out of the bed and sat on the chair. She tossed Emily her sweatshirt.

"They took this off of you while you were in the ambulance. They gave it to me when I got here."

"Thanks." Emily grinned. "You want to help me get dressed?" Her voice was playful.

"Hey, I have to tell you something," Micah said.

Emily sat up slowly. "Is being cryptic the new foreplay?"

Micah rolled her eyes and grudgingly entertained a smile. "For real, Em."

"Okay. For real. What is it?"

"Your mom came in here last night. You were asleep and she started talking to me."

"Was she rude to you?" Angst plagued Emily's eyes.

"No! Not at all. Emily, she kind of told me that she read a page of your journal. She knew, I guess, before last night, that you were gay."

Emily's face fell. "What? She read my journal?"

"She was worried."

"I don't care! She can't go around reading my stuff!"

"Look, I'm telling you this, because I thought you would like to know that you never really had a reason to be scared. She cares about you. Also, you shouldn't leave your journal lying around," Micah said, slowly looking up from the floor to meet Emily's gaze. She gave Emily a half-smile.

"Aargh! It's so hard to be angry around you! You're too friggin' cute," Emily whined.

"She wants to make up with you. Just hear her out."

Emily let out a sigh. "Fiiiine."

Micah stood up, walked to Emily, and gave her a kiss on the cheek. "Thank you."

"A kiss on the cheek? I *know* you can do better than that."

Just then the nurse walked in. "Emily?"

Emily raised her hand. "Here."

The nurse smiled. "How are you feeling today?"

Emily smiled back. "I'm hanging in."

"Good. Your mom is here, so let's see if we can get you home. I'm going to take out your IV and check your vitals."

"Okay, let's do this," Emily said.

The nurse took Emily's pulse, read her blood pressure, and took her temperature. When the nurse finished, she handed Emily some pamphlets.

"These will tell you everything you need to know about concussions and aftercare. If you should ever suffer another head injury, it's best to be checked out by a medical professional immediately as a precautionary measure. No more repeats of last night. Okay?"

Emily nodded and stared down at the medical literature she was holding. "Okay."

"You're all set then. Take care of yourself." The nurse smiled and left the room.

A minute later, Mrs. Mathis entered.

"Good morning, girls."

"Hey, Ma," Emily said.

"How are you feeling?" Mrs. Mathis asked.

"Better, thanks."

Mrs. Mathis smiled. "Are you ready to go home?"

"Yes!" Emily exclaimed. She turned to Micah and then back to her mother. "Mom, can I hang out with Micah later?"

Micah's eyes widened and she shook her head.

"We'll see, okay? Let's just get you home for now," Mrs. Mathis said.

Micah pointed to the door. "I should get a move on."

Emily reached out and took Micah's hand, heedless of attracting her mother's attention. "Wait! I'll see you later, right?"

Micah rubbed her thumb over Emily's knuckles and let go. "Call me after you get some rest."

"Believe me, I will." Emily smiled.

Micah smiled back and headed toward the door. She looked behind her. "Bye, Mrs. Mathis."

"Good-bye, Micah."

"Bye, Em."

"Bye!" Emily blew Micah a kiss and Micah mimed catching it. Emily laughed while Mrs. Mathis faked interest in the pamphlets on Emily's bed.

Micah gave one last wave and exited the room with Emily's intangible kiss in her hand.

Micah drove home from the hospital soundlessly. She walked into her house, which seemed eerily empty without her parents or Emily. Every room was dark because all the shades were still closed.

She turned on the kitchen light and went over to the fridge. She opened it and smiled at the plate of leftover pancakes. She didn't dare taint the keepsake. She sighed, closed the refrigerator, and made herself a peanut and butter and jelly sandwich. While she was eating, an idea formulated in her mind.

She scarfed down the rest of her food and hurried up the stairs. She dove into her closet and took an inventory of her formalwear. She stared for a long time at the single dress she owned.

Micah detested that dress. It had been given to her as a gift last Christmas. Her mom's smile had been grandiose as she handed Micah the silver-wrapped box. Micah had taken one look at the dress and scowled, then asked her mother to return it. Her mother had shrugged, said it came "from Santa," and that she had nothing to do with it. Mrs. Williams had explained that the shipping costs to the "North Pole" were beyond the family's budget. They never spoke of the dress again.

Micah touched the fabric and smiled. She then continued her search. Once she was satisfied with her findings, she went to take a shower.

She switched on the vanity lights in the bathroom and looked around. A spot of dried blood from when she had cut her hand blemished the edge of the tub. She scrubbed it off with a towel.

She undressed and viewed herself in the mirror. She saw that Emily had left a few marks on her body: one hickey on her inner right thigh and one on the lower left side of her waist. Micah smiled. She looked into her own eyes more closely. For the first time in a long time, Micah knew who was staring back at her.

"Welcome home," she said to her reflection. Disinclined to wipe away Emily's touch, she got in the shower anyway.

After she was dressed, Micah walked over to her stereo. She hit the "play" button, so that she could listen to the mix CD Emily had made for her. She smiled at the thought of the two of them dancing. She sang along to the songs as she pieced together the pages of their history project.

By the time she had organized everything, the music had stopped. She sat on her bed and tried to think of what else she could do to pass the time. Her phone rang. Micah answered right away.

"Hello?"

"Hi there. How's it going?" Emily asked.

"Good, I guess. How are you?"

"Okay. I'm kind of stuck here for the night. My parents want me to, get this, have a family dinner with them," Emily said in a tone of disbelief.

"That's cool. They're trying."

"I know, but I wanted to see you! I can't stop thinking about you. It's almost worse now that we're going out, because I actually *know* what I'm missing out on." Emily's voice indicated she was smiling.

"On the bright side," Micah responded, "my parents are going to be gone EVERY weekend for the next few weeks, sooooo…"

"Well, I've waited *this* long, so I guess a week won't kill me," Emily said.

"Look, I know you're stuck at home and all, but do you think your mom would mind if I came by just for a few minutes?" Micah asked.

"Why? What's going on?"

"Can you ask?"

"Yes, Micah, I'll ask. I'll text you back, okay?" Emily said.

"Nice! Thanks."

They hung up and a minute later Micah received a text from Emily that read, "See you soon."

Micah got what she needed and ran down the stairs. She headed out of the house and got into the car. She pulled up to Emily's house in no time. She took a deep breath and walked up to the front door. She rang the bell and listened.

Emily's father opened the door. "Micah," was all he said.

"Hi, Mr. Mathis."

Emily's mother appeared behind him. "Micah, come in."

Mr. Mathis opened the door and Micah forced a smile. "Thanks."

"She's in her room," Mrs. Mathis said.

Micah walked down the hallway and stopped at the last door on her right. She hadn't been in Emily's room in over a month. She knocked.

"Who is it?" Emily called through the door.

"Hot Megan," Micah called back.

Emily opened the door and smiled. "Quick, come in. My girlfriend will be here any minute!" Emily said in a rushed voice, pulling Micah into the room.

Micah started to laugh. She stopped as soon as Emily backed her up against the closed door and started kissing her. Micah gently pushed Emily away.

"Stop," she whispered. "Your parents!"

Emily smiled. "I know. I couldn't help myself. What's in the bag?" Emily pointed to the travel bag that Micah had been carrying.

Micah smiled and put the bag on the floor. She took Emily's hand.

"I have a serious question for you."

Emily laughed. "Micah, all of your questions are serious."

"Hey!"

"I'm kidding! What's your question?"

Micah bit her bottom lip and then reached inside the bag. She produced her dress.

"Emily, will you be my date to the Senior Gala?" Micah held out the dress for Emily to take.

"Yes!" Emily's face was aglow as she took the gown from Micah. "And you're sure you want to do this?"

"Absolutely." Micah smiled shyly. "Do you like it? I figured since we're the same size…"

"I love it! But what will you wear?"

"I've got it covered," Micah said. She gave Emily a quick kiss on the lips.

"Hey, my mom said you could stay for dinner," Emily said.

"I think maybe it's important that you do this one without me," Micah said, rubbing Emily's arm supportively.

"You're probably right."

"Listen, will you meet me in front of the school tomorrow morning? It might be easier if we—"

Emily cut Micah off. "We'll go in together. Don't worry."

Micah smiled. "Okay. I'll see you in the morning." Micah wrapped her arms around Emily. She held her close for a minute before backing away. Micah opened the door to leave.

"Micah?" Emily's voice was soft.

Micah turned to face her. "Yeah?"

Emily smiled and mouthed the words, "I love you."

Micah's body warmed throughout watching Emily's lips move to form those words.

"I love you, too," Micah mouthed back and closed the door behind her.

Micah's parents' car was already in the driveway when she got back home. She stared at the door, counted to three, and turned the handle with vigilance. She entered the house through the living room, hoping they would be in the kitchen and she could sneak up to her room. No such luck. Her parents were in the living room unpacking their suitcases.

Her mother looked up at the sound of the door closing and smiled. "Hi, sweetie. Where were you?" Mrs. Williams asked.

"Oh, I went over to check on Emily. She's resting. You guys are home early?"

Micah's dad walked over to her and gave her a hug. "We were worried about you, honey."

"Thanks, but I'm fine. You didn't have to come home."

Micah's mother laughed. "Don't sound too happy to see us. I thought that after last night, it would be nice for us to sit down together as a family and chill."

"Chill? You guys need to ease up on the slang. It's not working for either of you."

Mr. Williams laughed. "Sorry we're not dope enough."

Micah rolled her eyes, slouched on the sofa, and let out a long sigh.

"Rough night?" Mrs. Williams asked.

"Ugh. You have no idea! But I'm actually kind of glad you guys are home. I sort of need your help."

Micah's parents looked at one another.

"With what?" her mother asked.

Micah stood up. "I'm taking Emily to the Senior Gala. As my date." She braced herself.

Her father smiled and put out his palm to her mother.

"You owe me five bucks," he said.

"Damn it," Micah's mom mumbled.

"What? You guys were betting on my dating life?"

"It's the only thing we could do to keep from worrying," her mother explained.

Micah looked at her father. "You were betting on Emily?"

Her father smiled. "She makes you laugh more than the other girl."

"Casey." Micah tasted something bitter in her mouth saying the name aloud. Seemingly guilt had a flavor.

"Right. Well, it doesn't matter now anyway, does it?" Mr. Williams asked.

Micah shrugged. "I guess not?" She then shot her mother a questioning look.

Her mom nodded. "Yes, I rooted for the other girl. I knew things had been shaky between you and Emily, and I wanted that five bucks. Bad call on my part."

Micah tightened her lips. "I can't believe you two!"

Her parents began to laugh again.

"Sorry, Micah. We didn't mean to upset you," her mother said. "You know how much I like Emily."

Micah shook her head and cracked a smile. "So can you guys help me? Get ready for the dance? It's happening Friday."

"What do you need?" her mother asked.

"I need you to help me put together an outfit." Micah looked over at her dad. "And can you teach me how to tie a tie?"

Her father smiled. "I feel so privileged."

"Mom?" Micah glanced over at her mother.

"Why don't you just wear the dress you have? The one Santa got you?" her mother asked.

Both Micah and her father looked at her mother with their eyebrows raised.

Micah's mom held up her hands. "Alright! I know, I know." She smiled. "Of course I'll help."

"Besides, Mom. Emily's going to wear the dress."

Micah's mother beamed. "Oh, how lovely! At least *someone* appreciates my, I mean Santa's, sense of fashion."

Micah shook her head. "Riiight."

She walked over to her parents with her arms open and the three of them embraced.

"Thanks, you guys. I love you."

Chapter Twenty-Five

Micah and Emily stood outside of the high school Monday morning. They watched as crowds of students passed by them. *Soon they're all going to whisper and stare.* Micah looked over at Emily, who just nodded and smiled reassuringly.

The bell rang and they had four minutes left to get to homeroom. At this point, they were the only two people who had yet to enter the building.

"Are you ready?" Emily asked, holding out her hand.

Micah laced her fingers between Emily's. She brought their hands up to her mouth and kissed the back of Emily's.

"I'm ready."

They opened the front door to the building and made their way down the halls. Some kids did a double take at the two girls holding hands and a few of them snickered. But most students weren't even paying attention. *This isn't so bad*, Micah thought.

As they approached Micah's locker, they both stopped short at the sight of Jared Woods approaching them.

"Just keep walking," Emily counseled through the side of her mouth.

"Hello, ladies," Jared said, glancing down at their hands and smirking.

"Hello, Jared," Micah said, stopping. Emily rolled her eyes to let Micah know that she wished Micah had ignored him.

"We"—Jared began, moving his finger back and forth between himself and Emily—"could've been awesome together."

Emily let out a loud laugh, causing a few students to stop and watch. "Is that so?"

Micah tensed up and Emily squeezed her hand to anchor her.

"Well, we"—Emily was now motioning her finger back and forth between herself and Micah—"*are* awesome together, so get the fuck out of our way."

Micah grinned.

"Outing yourselves, huh?" he said, nodding slowly.

"I didn't want to give you the satisfaction," Emily explained.

Jared laughed. "Oh, this is much more gratifying. Now that I know you're together, I can daydream about the two of you."

Micah stepped forward, but Emily restrained her again.

"Don't," Micah said sharply, pointing her finger at him.

Jared didn't finish his sentence. He just winked at the two girls.

"Pervert," Micah mumbled.

"Dyke," Jared said in a much more audible tone than Micah had used.

There were a few more transient glimpses from students.

"And don't you forget it!" Micah said. Jared's expression lost all confidence. "Now you heard the girl. Get out of our fucking way."

The late bell went off. Teachers began ordering students to class. Jared stepped aside and kept walking.

Emily turned to Micah and smiled. "Nicely done!"

"Thanks." Micah shrugged. "This feels right, us. So I'm gonna fight for it."

Emily shook her head, smiling. "I want to kiss you so bad right now."

Micah smiled. "Get to class so you don't get in trouble." She gave Emily a nudge in the direction of Emily's homeroom, as she began walking towards her own.

"I'll see you at lunch?" Emily asked before disappearing completely.

"Count on it."

Micah entered her homeroom and most eyes were on her. *This is real. This is not a figment of your imagination. You can do this. Head down and keep walking.* Micah inhaled and let out a deep breath. She evaded Jared's middle finger, which was aimed at her. She sat down in her seat as the teacher called her name for attendance.

"Here," Micah said. A few students in the back of the room laughed quietly. *Were they taunting Emily in the next room over, too?*

Micah closed her eyes. She and Emily were at the playground. They were in a fort made of sofa cushions watching movies way past their bedtime. They were in Micah's room conveying their innermost thoughts and feelings on a dreary afternoon, a lazy weekend, a snow day. They were lying in Micah's bed together, spellbound. Micah opened her eyes. An unpleasant high school existence was something they would adapt to together. It was worth it. All of it. Besides, it was better than living a life of lies.

When it was time for first period, Micah searched the corridors for Emily, but was unable to spot her. She went to English class lacking the encouraging speech she had hoped to get.

Casey looked up as Micah sat down. Sam turned to face Micah and they stared at each other.

"What?" Micah asked in a hushed voice.

Sam shook her head. "So, is she up for grabs now?" Sam pointed behind her at Casey, who was pretending to listen to the teacher.

Micah's eyes opened wide. "Are you for real?"

"Just thought I would ask as a courtesy. You can't stop me anyway," Sam said, smiling.

An angry laugh escaped Micah, but it was only loud enough for Sam to hear. "I think you should stay away from her."

Without warning, Casey got up out of her seat. She looked over at Sam and then at Micah.

"And what are you? My knight in shining armor now?"

"Girls!" the teacher deplored. The whole class fell silent to watch.

"Casey. Shh. Not here," Micah appealed.

"Don't tell me to 'shoosh'! I didn't ask you to look out for me. I asked you to stay the hell out of my life!" Casey yelled.

"Casey! Principal's office. Now!" the teacher ordered.

"Whatever," Casey muttered. She quickly picked up her bag and left the room.

"Guys, eyes on the board," the teacher chided. Most of the students gave him their full attention.

"Smooth," Sam mumbled under her breath in Micah's direction.

Micah gave her a dirty look. This time she made sure Sam received it.

After class, Micah walked to the principal's office. Casey was sitting in the waiting area. Micah teetered in the doorway and then approached her.

"What the hell was that?" Micah asked.

Casey looked up. The rims around her eyes were red from crying. "GO. AWAY."

Micah sat down next to Casey.

Casey laughed through clenched teeth. "Jesus, Micah, leave me alone."

"I won't."

"Why? Why do you insist on pissing me off?" Casey shouted.

"Casey, you said I was unlike anyone you ever met, so let me be here for you!" Micah yelled back.

"Micah, when you break someone's heart, you can't be the one to comfort them." Casey began crying again. "It doesn't work that way."

Micah put her arms around Casey. "Please don't cry. Casey, I'm sorry."

Casey gave in and began to sob into Micah's shoulder. After a while, Casey gained control over herself and she looked up. Her face was close enough to Micah's that Micah could smell Casey's flavored lip gloss. Casey tilted her head and leaned in. Micah swallowed hard and backed away.

An angry voice pierced the air. "What are you doing?"

Both Micah and Casey jumped and turned to face the origin of the voice. Emily stood there. Her mouth opened, but no other words came out. Emily's eyes began to well up.

"Em, it's not what you think!" Micah lunged towards the doorway, where Emily was standing still. Micah reached for Emily, but Emily sidestepped.

"Emily, listen to her," Casey said, pointing to Micah.

Emily fixed her eyes sharply on Casey. "You. Shut your mouth." Emily faced Micah.

"Micah, I thought you said…" Emily stopped speaking, blinked resolutely, and shook her head. "You know what? Forget it," Emily said and turned to leave.

"Emily!" Micah called after her, but it was too late. Emily was gone.

Mr. Lewis stepped out of his office as the next period was beginning. He looked at Casey.

"Are you calm enough to go to your next class now?"

Casey nodded. "Yes, sir."

"Then get to class, girls. And stay OUT of trouble," he commanded.

Micah glared at Casey as the two of them left the principal's office and entered the hallway.

"Micah! I swear I didn't know she was there," Casey explained.

"Does it matter?" Micah asked. "You can't try to do stuff like that! We're not together, Casey." Micah let out a hostile laugh. "You're unbelievable! I was trying to be nice. I really *do* care about you, but I can't change the way I feel. I'm sorry that I hurt you and you can hurt me back. That's fine. But leave Emily out of this!"

Casey was left standing alone in the hall as Micah briskly walked away.

Throughout the course of the morning, Micah was on a quest for Emily. She panicked when she didn't see Emily at lunch. She left the cafeteria and scouted the girls' locker room. When Emily wasn't there either, Micah hightailed it to the library.

She scampered up the stairs towards the spot where she and Emily usually met. She turned the corner and saw Emily huddled up against the wall, crying. Micah sighed, a fusion of relief and agony. She knelt down in front of Emily, whose face was buried in her palms.

"Emily, I need you to look at me."

Emily groaned and glanced up, her eyes watery and dull. "What do you want?"

Micah held in her own tears. "You! Emily, I want you! Look, nothing happened. Casey tried to…"

"I know," Emily confessed.

Micah's brow pleated. "How?"

"Casey hunted me down. She caught up to me after my sociology class. She dragged me over to the fire exit and told me what happened," Emily explained. "Girl has a frickin tough grip."

Micah smiled a little. It was true. "What did she tell you exactly?"

Emily shrugged. "She told me that you were just...well, being yourself. She said you were trying to comfort her because you felt bad. And she tried to kiss you and you rejected her." Emily sighed. "She told me I'd be an idiot if I thought you would do that to me. She's right."

Micah put her hand against Emily's cheek. "Emily, if we're in this together like we said, then you have to trust me. You can't just run away. I'm your best friend and I can't believe you thought that I would..."

"Micah, I know. But that's the problem."

"What's the problem?"

"You're my best friend. You're my girlfriend. You're *everything* to me. You have been since I was a kid. All you would have to do is hurt me once and I would fall apart. That terrifies me!" Emily took a deep breath. "It's like I saw you there with her and it just hit me. The world of hurt I would be in if you were gone. It was surreal."

Micah leaned over and kissed Emily's cheek. "Emily, you do realize that I feel the same exact way about you? Don't you?"

"I guess I didn't think of it that way."

"Listen to me. I'm right here because this is where I want to be. It's like it's where I was meant to be."

Emily slowly began to smile. "I'm sorry I ran. I'm sorry that I doubted you, even though it was only for a second, because I do trust you."

"You know, you look hot in that outfit," Micah said, looking Emily up and down.

Emily shook her head. "You say things at the strangest times."

Micah shrugged. "Not true. Like when? Give me one example."

"When you asked me out at the *hospital*."

Micah frowned. "Okay, fine. Maybe that's my thing."

"Your thing?"

"Yeah, like my timing will be off. That will be my M.O." Micah said.

"Really? So you're—" Emily was intercepted when Micah forcefully pressed her mouth against hers. After a long kiss, Micah sat back on her knees, grinning proudly.

"Oh, I'm sorry. Was my timing off?" Micah asked.

"You have no idea how much I like your new M.O."

Micah stood up and pulled Emily up with her. "Let's get the rest of this day over with."

"I'd like that," Emily said, nodding. "And turn in our history project."

Micah radiated. "Totally! Four days early! Bam!" They high-fived each other and made their way back over to the school, arm in arm.

After the last bell of the day, Micah met up with Emily at her locker.

"We did it!" Emily announced.

"Indeed we did!"

"You ready to get out of this place?"

Micah noticed Casey walking by them through the corner of her eye. "Sure, do you mind if I…"

Emily looked over and saw Casey at her locker a few feet away. "I'll meet you outside."

"Thanks." Micah smiled and watched Emily leave the building, secretly enjoying the view from behind. When Emily was out of sight, Micah went up to Casey.

"Hey," Micah initiated.

Casey turned to her. "Hey."

"So Emily told me that you talked to her. She told me what you said."

"You're welcome, Micah," Casey said, smiling softly. "It's over now."

"Right." Micah nodded and walked away.

Emily looked up from where she was sitting on the grass as Micah neared.

"How'd it go?" Emily asked.

"I felt like I should thank her. I know it's weird, but it's—"

Emily put her finger over Micah's mouth. "It's who you are. It's one of the reasons why I'm sweet on you."

Micah smiled, her blush rising. "Aww, you're *sweet* on me, huh?"

Emily smiled back. "Don't mess me up. I'm trying to be romantic."

"You've succeeded. Can we go home now?"

"Yes, let's go home."

Chapter Twenty-Six

"How was your first week being out of the closet?" Micah's mother asked her as they stood in Micah's bedroom.

Micah looked at her mom and started to laugh. "You can just say being 'out.'"

"Well, excuse me!" Micah's mom said theatrically.

"It was okay. The first day was the hardest." Micah paused. "I think kids start getting tired of talking about the same people over and over, and then eventually find a new target."

Micah's mom smiled. "Ah yes. Some things don't change. It's tough being a teenager."

"That's an understatement."

"It's tough being an adult, too, though."

Micah nodded. "I can imagine."

"Your father and I, we're proud of you."

"For what?"

"Being who you are! And not taking anyone's shit," Micah's mom said.

"Mom! Language."

They both laughed as Mrs. Williams finished buttoning Micah's blouse. "That should do it."

Micah looked in the mirror. She had on charcoal pin-striped dress pants with a black button-up top. She looked behind her at the bedroom door.

"Dad! You're up!" Micah called to him.

Micah's dad walked into the bedroom holding a necktie. He smiled at Micah and Mrs. Williams.

"I'm here." He went over to Micah and swung the tie around her neck. "I'll show you how and then you can try, okay?"

"Okay."

Micah listened carefully as her father guided her through the instructions. She made her own attempt and got it right on the first try.

"Ta-da!" Micah exclaimed. Her parents laughed.

"Now give us a twirl," Micah's mother requested.

Micah rolled her eyes and twirled around. Her parents clapped.

"Oh! I forgot," Micah said and went into her closet. She pulled out a fedora hat and carefully situated it on her head. "Now I'm ready."

The doorbell rang and Micah's knees weakened. She glanced over to her mom. "That's probably Emily."

Micah's dad smiled. "I'll get the camera!" he said, rushing out of the room.

Micah's mother smiled at her. "Are you nervous?"

"A little," Micah admitted.

"Don't pay attention to anyone and have fun."

Micah hugged her mother. "Thanks, Mom."

"Let's go answer the door. You should never keep your date waiting."

"Got it," Micah said. She made her way down the stairs, her mother tailing behind her.

Micah stood in front of the door, took a deep breath, and opened it. Her heart stopped when she saw Emily. The black dress fit her perfectly, accentuating the outline of her body in all the right places. Her blonde hair was pulled up, with long strands purposefully hanging loose. She was holding a white rose. Micah was too busy checking out Emily to notice that Emily's mouth had dropped at the sight of Micah. Eventually they both realized that they were gawking at each other and they laughed nervously.

"You look amazing!" Emily broke the silence. "Oh. This is for you." Emily handed the rose to Micah.

Micah accepted the flower and smiled.

"Thanks, Em. You look"—Micah, enraptured, struggled to find words—"beautiful!"

Emily smiled humbly.

"Picture time!" Micah's dad hollered from behind.

Micah mouthed the word, "Sorry," to Emily.

"No worries."

Micah turned around to face her father and put her arm around Emily's shoulder. "Okay. Ready."

Micah's mother frowned. "Are you friends or are you on a date?"

Micah shot her mother a look. "We're BOTH actually."

"Fair enough," Micah's mother said agreeably. "Emily, how about you turn to the side?"

Micah groaned. "Mom!"

Emily laughed. "The more you complain, the longer this will last," she warned Micah. She turned to the side as she was told.

"And Micah, how about you stand behind Emily, since you're a little taller, and put your arms around her waist?" Micah's mom instructed. Then she asked Micah's father if he were ready. He nodded.

"Okay! Smile!" Micah's dad said loudly enough for the neighbors to hear.

"I so want to tear your clothes off," Micah whispered in Emily's ear as she innocently smiled up at the camera. Micah's words sent goosebumps over Emily's bare skin.

Micah's dad snapped two pictures.

"All set. You girls look marvelous!"

Mrs. Williams walked over to Micah and dropped the car keys in her palm.

"Home by eleven."

Micah nodded. "Home by eleven," she said. She took Emily's hand as they headed down the walkway.

Micah and Emily got in the car and started towards the school auditorium. At every stop light, Micah stole a glance at Emily.

"Micah, the fedora really works for you," Emily said through a grin. "And so does the tie."

Micah smiled. "I thought you might like it."

"You thought right." Emily was flustered.

Micah pulled up to another red light and looked at Emily. "I'm so glad I gave that dress to you."

"Oh? Did you mean what you said back at your parents'?" Emily asked, giving Micah's tie a light tug.

"Um, yeah I did."

Emily laughed as Micah began driving again. "Are you scared? About the dance?"

"I was. But since you showed up at my door looking like *that*, I haven't really been thinking about anything else." Micah was shaking her head, chuckling.

They arrived at the school. Micah parked the car in a reclusive area in the back of the building. "Here we are." She unfastened her seatbelt.

"Wait," Emily petitioned. She snagged the length of Micah's necktie and used it to rope Micah in closer.

"I like this," Emily said, glancing down at the tie. "It works to my advantage."

Micah let Emily pull her in. She had been craving the taste of Emily's lips all day. She craned her neck slightly so that her mouth was barely touching Emily's, tantalizing her, before she kissed Emily passionately. Emily's hands fumbled with the buttons of Micah's shirt as Micah's hand made its way up Emily's dress. Micah started to laugh.

"Okay, we need to control ourselves," Micah suggested. Emily started to nibble on Micah's earlobe, which only excited Micah more. She began kissing Emily again with a hunger that she didn't even realize existed within herself.

Then Emily started laughing. "I'm sorry. You were saying something about controlling ourselves?"

Micah put her forehead on Emily's shoulder. "This is going to be a long night."

"It sure is, but we'll get through it," Emily said. "Now, you have to back up or I'm going to continue to fight those buttons on your shirt. That's a fight I'm not going to lose."

Micah grinned and buttoned up her shirt. "Are we the first gay couple to go to Senior Gala?"

Emily thought for a minute. "We might be?"

"Let's show them what we got," Micah said, stepping out of the car. She walked over to the passenger side and opened the door for Emily.

"Why, thank you," Emily said, placing her hand in Micah's. They headed for the entrance.

Inside, the auditorium was decorated with colorful streamers and balloons. Couples were dancing to the surprisingly tasteful music.

Micah led Emily over to the punch bowl. "Want some?" Micah asked, nodding to the punch.

"No, thanks. I'm good."

They stood side-by-side at the table. A few of their classmates stopped and stared at the sight of Emily's arm around Micah's waist. Most of them, however, were too invested in the festivities to take note. Micah and Emily had been openly dating for only a week, but to the senior class, this was just a minor shift in dynamics. Micah and Emily were almost always together anyway.

The song changed to something of a slower pace. Lulling vocals harmonizing with a piano filled the room. This song was on the mix that Emily had recently made for Micah. Micah took Emily's arm from her waist and stood in front of Emily.

"What's wrong?" Emily asked.

Micah smiled. "Nothing's wrong. I'm cashing in on that favor you owe me."

"Now?"

Micah held out her hand. "May I have this dance?"

The corners of Emily's mouth drew upwards in a smile that could've lit up the room on its own. She put her hand in Micah's.

"This is a big step for you. You got this?"

Micah smiled and gently drew Emily closer until their bodies were pressed against each other.

"I've got this," Micah said confidently. "You see, my arm goes here like this," Micah said, putting her arm around Emily's neck. Micah continued, "And your hand goes here." Micah placed Emily's hand on her waist. Micah held Emily's other hand in her own. "And now you just follow my lead."

Even in the darkened auditorium, Micah could tell that Emily was gushing.

"Always," Emily said.

"Always what?" Micah asked, smiling at her.

"I will always follow your lead."

Micah kissed Emily softly on the lips and then rested her cheek against Emily's. An incredible happiness filled Micah's heart, and she smiled as a tear trickled down her face.

"Are you crying?" Emily asked softly.

"Yes. Because I love you."

"I love you, too, Micah."

As the song came to an end, Micah and Emily continued swaying back and forth, holding each other tightly. Neither of them had any intentions of letting go.

The end

Made in the USA
Lexington, KY
02 December 2013